ENLIGHTENED

David Lauriston has been recuperating at Lord Murdo Balfour's Laverock estate for the last five months. At Laverock, he has regained his health and confidence and has found—with Murdo—more happiness and contentment than he has never known before.

David is all too aware that some day soon he will have to leave Laverock—and Murdo—and return to his legal practice in Edinburgh, just as Murdo will have to return to his life in London. But when David's mentor, Patrick Chalmers, asks David to return to Edinburgh to visit him on his deathbed, it seems that day has come sooner than either David or Murdo would have wished.

Chalmers begs David to undertake one last piece of business for him: to secure the future of Chalmers's daughter Elizabeth. But to carry out his old mentor's wishes, David must travel to London, with Murdo.

No sooner have the two men arrived in the capital than they encounter Murdo's ruthlessly manipulative father, who reveals a shocking secret that rocks David to his foundations. What's more, when David discovers Elizabeth is facing far greater danger than even her father feared, he is determined to help her, no matter the cost to his own safety.

As the stakes rise, it is Murdo who must choose what he is prepared to sacrifice to keep David at his side, and ask whether there is any possibility of lasting happiness for men like them.

ENLIGHTENED

JOANNA CHAMBERS

JOANNA CHAMBERS BOOKS

Copyright © 2017 Joanna Chambers

2nd edition

Cover art: Natasha Snow

Editor: Linda Ingmanson

Published by Joanna Chambers

Digital ISBN: 978-1-9997091-2-9

Print ISBN: 978-1548176334

All rights reserved. This book or any portion thereof may not be used, reproduced or transmitted in any form or by any means without express written permission of the publisher.

This is a work of fiction. All characters, places and events in this book are fictitious. Any resemblance to actual persons, living or dead, or business establishments or organisations is completely coincidental.

Dedication

For my boys

CHAPTER ONE

February 1823, Perthshire

"What do you say, Mr. McNally? It's a generous offer."

McNally considered, the furrows on his brow deep as a new-ploughed field, while David watched him, waiting patiently for a response. McNally's craggy face was weather-beaten from years spent outside, and his clothes were plain and homely. He was no gentleman farmer, but David did not underestimate him. The man was successful and canny. He'd tripled the size of his holdings over the last ten years, and the yields he achieved were consistently good, far better than any of his neighbours'.

"So, His Lordship's just goin' tae let me have the whole o' that west field?" he said now, his frown sceptical.

David nodded. "As I said, His Lordship wishes to bring the court case to an end and to repair neighbourly relations. He is willing not only to give up all claims to the west field but to convey his own share to you.

All he asks in return is that you abandon your dispute over the boundary line to the south."

"Perhaps I'm not minded tae give up that claim," McNally said carefully, watching David.

David smiled. "Now, Mr. McNally, you know and I know that it's a bad claim." When McNally opened his mouth to protest, David added smoothly, "But His Lordship understands why you raised it. You were defending yourself against Sir Hamish. It's perfectly understandable."

The late Sir Hamish Muir had raised the court action against McNally a decade ago. The present owner, Lord Murdo Balfour, who had purchased the Laverock estate in its entirety from Sir Hamish's beleaguered executors two years previously, had discovered its existence only a few months ago, when David had begun to slowly piece together the great, disorganised mess that was Sir Hamish's private papers.

It had certainly explained the black looks and stony silences that McNally had been sending Murdo's way all this time.

"Ye're right I was defendin' myself," McNally said, wagging a finger at David. "Fight fire with fire, that's what my old man always said. And it's cost me awful dear in this case, Mr. Lauriston, awful dear!"

"Which is why His Lordship is prepared to offer twenty-five pounds toward the costs you have incurred," David said, playing his final card.

"Twenty-five pound?"

McNally's surprise at that offer was plain. David smiled and waited.

Sir Hamish had been not merely quarrelsome with his neighbours, he had been a litigious old bugger who'd served a dozen writs in the last decade of his life, claiming to own plots of land here, there and everywhere. Over the last month, David had brought most of the festering disputes to an end by simply withdrawing the case in question and offering an olive branch to the other party in the form of an invitation to tea with His Lordship. There were a few, however, like this one with McNally, that were trickier. Cases where the other party had counterclaimed, as McNally had, when Sir Hamish had tried to establish that he owned not merely half of the west field at the edge of the Laverock estate, but the whole of it.

It was the worst sort of nonsense. The truth was, the field in question was nothing but a rocky bit of upland. It was suitable only for sheep to graze on, and Murdo already had plenty of land like that, most of which was far more convenient and had better grazing than the godforsaken corner of the world that was the west field. Worse, the boundary wall going down the middle of the field was falling into disrepair after ten years of neglect and needed replacing. In short, it was nothing to Murdo to give away his half of the field. To

McNally, though, it was a victory against Sir Hamish. Particularly when sweetened with twenty-five pounds toward McNally's lawyer's bills.

"Done," McNally said, thrusting out his hand. "The truth is, I'd fair like tae see the back o' that court case meself. I've had enough o' lawyers tae last me a lifetime, Mr. Lauriston. Nae offence."

David took McNally's hand and shook it. "None taken, Mr. McNally. His Lordship will be pleased you agreed to his proposal. And he is keen to get to know his neighbours better. Would you and your wife agree to dine at Laverock House on Wednesday evening? The Blairs are coming."

McNally's brows went up at that. "Has he settled with old man Blair an' all? Last time I spoke to Willie Blair, he told me there was nothin' Lord Murdo could offer that he'd bite at."

David just smiled. "Well now, that's something you'll have to ask Mr. Blair about," he said, rising from his chair. His leg protested with a shaft of pain, but he schooled his expression to show no discomfort. "So, may we expect you and Mrs. McNally on Wednesday?"

"Aye, then, what time shall we come?"

"Does six o'clock sound all right?"

"Six o'clock," McNally agreed, nodding. "Come on and I'll show ye out, Mr. Lauriston."

McNally was in a better mood on David's way out

than on his way in. He introduced his wife and three daughters, who were sewing in the parlour, and gave him a brief tour of the farm buildings outside the farmhouse, including his new dairy. It was a good farm, tidy, well kept and industrious. It reminded David of his father's farm, though this was much bigger.

When he made a comment to that effect, McNally warmed up even more.

"Ye were a farm boy, then?"

"Born and bred." David smiled.

"I knew there was a reason I liked ye." McNally grinned, clapping him on the shoulder. "All the lawyers I met before were as stiff as if they had poles up their arses. Why did ye decide to become one of them?"

"I have an older brother," David offered, "so he'll get the farm." That wasn't the whole explanation, not really, but it seemed to satisfy McNally.

"Ah well," McNally said as he showed David out the door, his tone heavy with sympathy, "it seems ye've found yer way back to the country now, Mr. Lauriston. It's a good man o' business you are, tae His Lordship."

David smiled and thanked the man, enduring a punishingly enthusiastic handshake before taking his leave. By now, his leg was aching badly, but he made himself walk straight, concealing his weakness as he walked down the track from the farmhouse to the first of the stiles he would have to climb over on his way back to Laverock House.

Though he knew McNally would likely have lost interest and turned away, he determinedly kept up his charade, smothering a wince when he stepped off the stile onto his bad leg and setting off again, concentrating on keeping his gait straight and regular.

He knew he'd overdone it. He'd known it by the time he was two-thirds of the way to McNally's house this morning. He'd known it as he sat in McNally's parlour, his knee throbbing with hot needles of pain, wishing he'd abandoned his pride and brought the fancy cane Murdo had given him a fortnight before. But it had seemed a perfectly reasonable decision when he'd set out this morning.

The four months of inactivity with his leg splinted and harnessed had driven him nearly mad. Since getting the harness off, he'd been gradually increasing the length of his daily stroll, eager to build the muscles again. His leg was getting stronger every day, and when he'd risen this morning, he'd felt very ready for the two-mile walk to McNally's house.

He'd seriously underestimated what he was undertaking.

Until today, he'd been sticking to well-worn tracks and roads on his walks. But the route to McNally's stretched across field after field of hilly, uneven ground that jarred his leg with every step.

He'd thought to himself this morning that two miles was nothing, but it hadn't felt like nothing when he'd reached McNally's farmhouse, and it didn't feel like nothing now as he reached the top of the field that Sir Hamish and McNally had been arguing about, and climbed yet another stile. His hip protested as he pulled himself up and his knee ached like the very devil, but there was nothing for it but to thole it now. Thole it, and keep going till he got back to Laverock House.

There had been a hard frost overnight and the ground had no give in it. It felt like iron under David's feet, punishing him for his foolishness. The day was cold too, even now, late in the afternoon. David's breath flowered white out of his mouth as he puffed his way up to the top of the next field, cresting a hill that gave him a view over Laverock Glen. He paused there, looking out at the broad sweep of the dun-coloured winter hills, the silver ribbon of the river, glittering where it broke over jagged rocks. And the sight eased something in David, soothing him the way the weak winter sun soothed the landscape with its gentle light.

He took the descent slowly, forced to it by the pain in his knee. The view was a sop to Cerberus, something good to distract him from the pain. He paused several times on the way down, leaning his weight on a bit of wall or a tree when he got the chance.

When he reached the bottom of the hill and got onto the blessedly level path that wound through the glen to Laverock House, he was ready to weep from relief. Yet there was still half a mile to go.

He took it slowly. By halfway, he'd have given his left arm for the cane he'd thrown aside this morning. Anything to take some of the burden from his leg. Ah well, he was a fool, and he'd learned something today. Maybe he'd listen to Murdo next time.

Murdo wouldn't be happy about today's events. He'd brought David to Laverock House to recuperate and was continually lecturing him about taking things easier. It was Murdo who'd arranged for the physician to come every few weeks to check how David's leg was healing, and who'd instructed the kitchen to make up regular batches of David's mother's liniment recipe. Murdo who'd presented David with a new ebony cane with a silver derby handle to take on his walks.

It wasn't only David's physical well-being that Murdo looked after. He'd had boxes of books brought to Laverock House from his Edinburgh townhouse to keep David amused; he'd even read to David himself in those early days when, listless and melancholy with his lot, David hadn't been inclined to do so. And it was Murdo who'd brought him Sir Hamish's papers to look through when, as his leg began to improve, he'd complained about needing something to test his wits on.

Now, that project had seized David's attention to such an extent that he was becoming known locally as Lord Murdo Balfour's very efficient new man of business, the learned lawyer who was helping Lord Murdo make peace with all his new neighbours and bury all the old disputes Sir Hamish had started.

And why not let them think that? It was true, after all—and it was no one else's concern that, besides that, he and Murdo were lovers. That was their affair and theirs alone. The servants at Laverock House certainly appeared to be oblivious. The manor was a good size, but it was compact enough that the proximity of their bedchambers, with only Murdo's untidy study between them, merited no comment.

By day, they were circumspect. By night—well, the nights were their own. It hadn't been easy to make love with David's injured leg—for months he'd been all but immobilised by the leg harness—but with a bit of inventiveness, they'd managed, and now that David was up and about again, it was getting easier every day.

Right now, though, as David took the last turn-off that led to Laverock House and the manor house finally hoved into view, he couldn't think of doing anything but lying down. He was limping badly now, all attempts to conceal his disability long given up. The idea of sinking into his soft featherbed and warming his chilled feet under the blankets had become his Holy Grail. There was simply nothing else.

He'd barely taken a dozen steps down the long front drive when the door opened and a tall, broad-shouldered man emerged.

Murdo.

Even now, after living here for months, the unexpected sight of his lover lit something inside David. He felt a stab of pure happiness, an accompanying flare of anticipation, even as he winced with each step he took.

"Where have you been?" Murdo said, walking toward him, his dark eyes concerned as he took in David's pronounced limp. "Mrs. Inglis said you went out hours ago."

David attempted a smile, but it felt more like a grimace. "I decided to walk over to McNally's," he admitted, sending Murdo a rueful look. "It wasn't one of my best ideas."

"That's over two miles!" Murdo exclaimed. He turned so that they were walking in the same direction, toward the open front door, matching his pace to David's. "What were you thinking? And where's your cane?"

"I didn't think I needed it," David mumbled, answering the second question and evading the first.

"You're limping," Murdo observed unnecessarily.

"I overdid it, but I'll be all right," David replied. "I just need to rest my leg for a bit."

Murdo let out a noisy sigh. "You're as stubborn as a

mule. I only hope you haven't set yourself back with this."

There were three steps up to the front door of the house, and David took them slowly, gritting his teeth against the pain that knifed through his knee with each step. He didn't look at Murdo, but he felt the other man's eyes on him, watching his slow progress and scrutinising his profile for evidence of how bad the pain was.

They stepped into the hallway together, Murdo closing the front door behind them. Since the hall was empty of servants, David allowed Murdo to help him off with his greatcoat. Then he glanced up the long flight of steps that led to his bedchamber on the first floor and suppressed a moan. Girding himself, he placed his foot on the first step.

"Don't even think about it," Murdo said behind him.

Before David could protest, Murdo was sliding one arm round David's back and the other under his knees, sweeping his feet out from under him. David hissed a curse as Murdo lifted him, but Murdo just shifted David's weight to balance himself and began to quickly mount the stairs.

"Christ, Murdo," David said testily. "Let me down, will you?" It had been a few weeks since he'd had to submit to this particular indignity. He hated being carried like this—it unmanned him.

Murdo ignored him, and after the first few stairs, despite his mortification, David didn't bother protesting any further. The truth was, he couldn't get up these stairs without Murdo's help.

By the time they reached the top, Murdo's breath was coming hard, but he still didn't let David down. He carried him another dozen steps to David's bedchamber door before setting his feet back on the ground. Even then he wasn't done. Steering David into his room, he guided him firmly to the featherbed David had been dreaming of for the last half hour, then went back to close the bedchamber door, turning the key in the lock. Returning to the bed, mouth set in a firm, determined line, he bent to remove David's boots. This time David didn't say anything. It would do no good, and anyway, he was bloody exhausted. So he let Murdo ease the tight leather from his calves, then slowly strip away the rest of his clothing, piece by piece.

"Do you want me to ring for a bath?" Murdo asked as he peeled away David's trousers, easing the fabric carefully down his legs so as not to jar him.

"I doubt I could climb in right now," David admitted.

"A rubdown with some liniment, then?"

David couldn't suppress the groan that emerged from his chest at that suggestion. "Please."

"Lie back, then. I'll strip down too."

David did as instructed, passively watching as Murdo removed his elegant clothing, then crossed the room, naked, to fetch the jar of liniment from the armoire, his tall, powerful body beautiful in the late afternoon light that seeped into the room round the edges of the drapes.

Murdo knelt beside David on the bed and regarded his leg. "Let's see what you've done to yourself."

Weary to the bone, David let his eyes close. Moments later, the drifting scents of rosemary and camphor heralded the opening of the liniment. It was a scent with which David was very familiar—his mother had been making the stuff for years, ever since his father had taken a tumble off the roof of the barn at home and injured his shoulder. The smell of it now brought with it the promise of imminent relief.

The brisk noise of Murdo rubbing the stuff between his palms brought the scent forth again, more intensely, as it warmed on Murdo's skin. And when Murdo laid his hands on David, every remaining thought in David's head vanished. Murdo's hands were strong and warm, their firm course eased by waxy lanolin and camphor oil as they broke into the knotted agony in David's leg and straightened him out again.

David could barely keep his eyes open by the time Murdo was finished. He felt languorous and done in, like he could sleep the rest of the day and night away. Somehow, though, he managed to crack open his eyelids and smile at Murdo, who was kneeling at his side, watching him.

"Thank you," David said softly.

"Better?" Murdo's smile was tender.

"Much."

"You look tired."

"Not *too* tired," David replied.

Murdo grinned and crawled over to lie beside David. He bent his head, capturing David's lips in a soft kiss that slowly deepened, while his hand drifted in light, teasing caresses, pausing for an instant to pinch at the tight bud of David's left nipple, making him moan his pleasure into the kiss.

"Careful," he murmured as David turned onto his side, worming his way closer.

"I'll be fine so long as I keep the weight off this leg," David replied, swooping in for another kiss. He drove his tongue deep into Murdo's mouth and let his own hands wander, loving the way Murdo's body shuddered and rolled under his fingers, loving the hitches of breath and low moans that came from Murdo's lips.

Much as he wanted this to last, his blood was up, and it seemed Murdo's was too. They began the familiar drag and thrust, the grinding circle of hips and dizzying friction of skin on skin. After a minute, Murdo broke their kiss and dropped his mouth to David's neck, sucking at the tender flesh there, grazing

David with his sharp teeth. David's head went back in surrender, and he groaned loudly.

"Yes. God, that's good," he hissed.

It could only have been seconds later when he felt the surge of his climax. It churned in his balls, then splattered in thick, hot pulses between them, coating their bellies, and an instant later, Murdo toppled too, his semen mingling with David's own.

They lay there kissing for long minutes after, warm and contented, stickily soiled. Despite the pain of his hard-won recuperation, these last months had been the best of David's life, and at times like these, lying in Murdo's arms, he still felt a dizzying sort of disbelief, both at his own happiness and at Murdo's.

After a while, Murdo slipped out of bed to clean himself up. He poured water into the ewer, yelping at the coldness of the washcloth on his warm belly, making David chuckle, then laugh harder when the other man advanced on him with the cold, damp cloth in his hand and a wicked grin on his face. David tried to squirm away, and they tussled briefly, laughing and kissing, till they were both clean and Murdo finally tossed the cloth aside and drew the blankets snugly around them.

"So," he said. "Did McNally accept the offer?"

David chuckled; he couldn't believe he'd forgotten to tell Murdo about his triumph.

"He made a show of reluctance, but I could tell

from the moment I mentioned settling things that he wanted to see the back of the case." David sent Murdo a challenging look. "I'm fairly sure he'd have come around without paying any costs to him."

"You still don't think I should have offered him any money," Murdo observed, seeming amused.

David considered that. "No," he said at last, relenting. "You were right. I think he'd have taken the offer without the money, but this way you showed yourself to be a fair and generous man—everything that Sir Hamish wasn't—and I suppose twenty-five pounds isn't so very much to pay for restoring relations with your nearest neighbour. Not for you anyway."

Murdo grinned. "You admit I was right, then?"

David rolled his eyes. "I wouldn't go that far. Let's just say I can understand your reasoning."

Murdo laughed softly and brushed a kiss over David's lips. He gave a sigh of contentment, a happy sound that made David's heart feel full and tender.

"Dr. Logan's coming up from Perth on Friday," Murdo murmured. "Make sure you tell him about what happened today."

David sighed. "It's not necessary to keep bringing him here every month. Not anymore. I'm nearly fully recovered. In fact—"

"You're far from fully recovered," Murdo interrupted. "As you've proved very well today."

"*In fact*," David repeated, his light tone belying the

heavy dread in his gut, "I'm probably well enough to go home." After a pause, he added, "To Edinburgh," as though Murdo might not understand precisely where he meant.

It was a topic that had been brewing for a while now—the last few weeks at least.

Murdo's lips thinned into a grim line. "Let's not talk about that now."

"When, then?"

There was a long silence, then Murdo said, his tone grudging, "After the physician's been."

Friday.

David sighed. Perhaps to Murdo it sounded like impatience. In truth, it was pure relief. Relief that this had been put off for another few days.

"All right," he agreed, resting his head on Murdo's broad shoulder. "Friday."

Chapter Two

By Thursday, David's leg still didn't feel much better, and it worried him. Had he damaged himself irreparably? Dr. Logan had been pleased with David's progress on his last visit, and, for the first time, David had allowed himself to hope that he might actually make a full recovery from his accident. The thought that he might have thrown that away, and through his own stupidity, ate at him.

To take his mind off it, he turned to work. Work had always been a refuge for him, and at Laverock House, there was plenty to be done. Over the last few months, bit by bit, Murdo had divulged to David his various and many business interests. He owned a coal mine in South Lanarkshire and a half share of a cotton mill in Sheffield. He had investments in canals and factories. He underwrote insurance arrangements and financed merchant ships. And there were always new opportunities being offered to him. It was well known that his support for a venture would draw more investors. His name was associated with success and security, and it lured others.

David was fascinated by it all—intrigued by the legal arrangements, appalled by the risks, amazed by the rewards. His involvement had begun with no more than mere dinner conversation, when he asked Murdo what kept him holed up in his study for so long. Soon, though, curiosity piqued, he was asking to look over the contracts and proposals Murdo was working on, and then, as he questioned Murdo about the workings of the schemes he was involved in, he found himself making notations, suggesting revisals and innovations. At first, his suggestions were tentative, but when Murdo showed interest in what he was saying and even grew excited by his ideas, David's confidence grew.

It wasn't long before Murdo raised the topic of money. When David balked at the idea of a salary, Murdo decided that a commission would be a better form of remuneration in any event. Four percent of returns, he'd decided, unilaterally. That way David could rest assured that his rewards would be commensurate with the success of the venture.

Once that had been sorted, Murdo really began to draw David in, giving David access to all his business correspondence and setting up a second desk in the study of Laverock House. Their working arrangements, which till now had been somewhat loose and sporadic, settled into a steady pattern of several hours most days, though the work was done at all different times of day, depending on what other commitments Murdo had.

Today, Murdo had business to attend to in Perth, so they agreed to spend an hour or two going through Murdo's bulging correspondence tray first thing, before taking a late, hearty breakfast, which would sustain Murdo till his return.

They started early, at seven, a pot of coffee on the desk between them as they pored over documents and letters in companionable silence.

"What does this say?" Murdo asked David after a while, showing him a scratched notation David had made in the margin of a fairly advanced proposal.

David took the paper he held out and peered at his own handwriting for a moment before the light dawned. "Oh, it says 'consider trust'. I was thinking that if the proceeds of sale were placed directly in trust, the trustees could be left to deal with ascertaining the dividends and paying them out to the investors. I thought that may alleviate your concerns about the funds being tied up if the Healey brothers start arguing amongst themselves again. The trustees will be able to release your share, and the Healeys can waste their shares on lawyers if they wish."

Murdo grinned, his left cheek dimpling and his eyes dancing with humour. "A neat solution," he agreed. "I shouldn't like to miss out on what promises to be a profitable venture, merely because the two principals argue like cat and dog."

David couldn't help but grin back, caught fast by that rare smile. It touched him, oddly, to see Murdo like this. So engaged and interested in what he was doing. When David first met Murdo, he hadn't seen this side of him. He'd seen only a supercilious aristocrat with a perpetual expression of cool amusement on his face, as though everyone he looked at was slightly below his notice. It had taken a while for the mask to crack, and even now, these moments of unreserved excitement were rare enough that they made David's heart beat a little quicker.

Murdo got like this about the estate too. His plans for the home farm at Laverock covered a three-year period, with every detail costed to the shilling. And he'd been systematically reviewing his tenants' properties since last winter, making notes of changes and improvements to be brought about. All this and wooing the neighbours too. Business was the man's element. He had a gift for it, a nose for profit and a mind like a trap.

On an impulse, David asked, "What does your father think about all this? The moneymaking, I mean."

Murdo's grin faded. He never spoke about his father and generally avoided any discussion of his family. What little David had managed to draw out of him suggested there were few good feelings, certainly on Murdo's side.

"My father despises all trade," he said. "But he needs it too. As a politician, he's more interested in power than wealth, but he needs to keep his personal coffers healthy to maintain his reputation as man of a means. He likes that I excel at something, but he would prefer me to turn my energies to politics rather than wasting it on making money." Murdo shrugged. "And he doesn't relish the taint of trade. Investments are all very well, but to actually engage in business is rather too much for him."

David couldn't help it—he laughed. Murdo's expression immediately lightened, his smile returning even as he frowned in puzzlement.

"What?" he said.

"It's so *absurd*," David replied. "This idea that work—business—is somehow shameful. As though the highest state to which a man may aspire is to be entirely idle."

"True. Though I cannot accuse my father of idleness, at least," Murdo said. "He has lived and breathed politics all his life. And he has spent the last twenty years trying to drag me along in his footsteps."

"Do you think you'll ever grant his wish?"

For a long moment, Murdo was silent.

"I don't plan to," he said at last. "But my father has a way of bending people to his will. He finds your weak spot, and he exploits it."

"Do you have weak spots to exploit, then?"

It was an impertinent question—none of David's business. But he wanted to know the answer.

"Everyone has weak spots," Murdo replied, giving David a careless smile. "The trick is not letting on what they are."

"That's not really an answer," David observed. He smiled, though he felt strangely disappointed in Murdo's careful response.

"Even my father has a weak spot," Murdo said.

"What is it?"

Murdo shrugged. "I don't know yet, but I mean to find out, one of these days."

An hour later, they were taking breakfast together when one of the maidservants popped her head round the door to say that Dr. Logan had just called by.

Murdo bade her show the physician in, and when the man entered, he looked weary and apologetic.

"I'm sorry to call so early, my lord," he said, "but I was attending the birthing of your neighbour's child till an hour ago and thought I'd take the chance of calling in on my way home in the hope that Mr. Lauriston may be willing to rearrange our appointment to save me coming back tomorrow." He turned to David. "Would that inconvenience you, Mr. Lauriston?"

"Of course not," David replied. "It suits me very well, in fact." He'd had to suppress a grimace at the stabbing pain that shuddered down his leg when he and Murdo rose to greet the doctor, but now he managed a smile as he shook the man's hand.

"Come and sit down, Doctor," Murdo invited the physician. "Could you manage some breakfast before you examine Mr. Lauriston? We've plenty here."

Logan readily agreed and was soon tucking into a plate of smoked haddock and eggs.

"I envy you your cook, my lord," he confided between mouthfuls. "She's a hundred times better than the fellow Sir Hamish had."

"Mrs. Inglis has been with me for many years."

The doctor showed his appreciation by scoffing a second helping of eggs, two bannocks and half a pot of coffee before he finally put down his napkin and sat back in his chair, a contented expression on his face.

"Well now, Mr. Lauriston," he said, "if you've finished your own breakfast, shall we repair to your bedchamber and see how this leg of yours is doing?"

"It's probably best if you examine Mr. Lauriston down here," Murdo interrupted before David could so much as open his mouth to speak. David pressed his lips together, irritated at Murdo's high-handedness but unwilling to argue in front of Dr. Logan with a man the good doctor believed was David's employer.

Logan turned to Murdo with a questioning look on his face.

"Mr. Lauriston overexerted himself on Monday," Murdo explained without so much as a glance in

David's direction. "He is still feeling the ill effects of his enthusiasm today—it may be better if you examine him in the sitting room next door to save him a painful walk upstairs."

"There's really no need—" David began.

"No, no. His Lordship is quite right, Mr. Lauriston," Logan said, turning to fix David with a stern look. "There's no use putting your leg under more stress for the sake of pride. His Lordship's sitting room will do perfectly well as an examination room. Lead the way, my lord."

Given leave to take charge, Murdo had no hesitation in taking the physician up on his invitation. David and Logan followed him out of the dining room and into the neighbouring sitting room, neither of them commenting when he made no move to leave them alone, but instead closed the door, then crossed the room to draw the drapes.

For an instant, David considered asking Murdo to leave. He hadn't stayed for any of David's other examinations, and David couldn't help but think it was unorthodox. But Murdo had a mulish expression on his face that David didn't like the look of, and Dr. Logan seemed to find the situation entirely unexceptionable.

"If you could strip down to your shirt and drawers, Mr. Lauriston," he said as he removed his coat and rolled up his shirtsleeves.

David did as he asked. He sent Murdo a warning look when the other man started to step forward to assist David with his right boot—always the most troublesome part of dressing and undressing for him—and then had to struggle with removing it for a good few painful seconds before he finally shook his foot free. Other than that, though, he got himself down to his underclothes with relative ease and lowered himself onto the chaise longue.

Logan drew up a footstool and perched on it. His forehead was lined in concentration, his attention all on David's leg. He asked David to lift the leg, move it outwards, flex it, straighten it. He examined every inch of it, from David's hip down to his foot. He checked the knee that had been giving David so much trouble despite the fact that neither one of his actual fractures had been anywhere near it. He ran his hands down the length of David's limb, his head cocked to one side in a way that made it look as though he was listening or thinking maybe, perhaps imagining the layers of bone and muscle and tissue inside. He had David stand and walk, then attempt a squat, noting aloud the last was still beyond him. He questioned David about his activities over the last month, most particularly about Monday's walk, over which he clucked and frowned in disapproval, making David feel like a naughty schoolboy.

When it was all over and David was pulling his

trousers back on, Logan gave his verdict.

"Well, Mr. Lauriston," he said, "despite your foolishness, your leg continues to heal well. You can bear your weight readily and the bones have knit as neatly as any I've ever seen—you must have had a good bonesetter see to it at the first. It's hard enough to get one fracture to set that well, never mind two."

"What about the limp? I still get it at times, when my leg gets tired."

"I hope it will disappear, in time, but I won't lie to you. There's a chance it will be permanent. Particularly if you don't take care of yourself properly. You must ensure that you don't damage the healing your leg's already done by engaging in any more nonsense like strenuous hillwalking before you've had more time to repair. At this point in time, you should be keeping your exercise to a gentle stroll of no more than a mile or so at a time over flat ground, gradually building up the distance and strenuousness over time. Avoid stressing the limb at all costs." He smiled then, his expression part sympathetic, part amused. "I've been a physician for twenty-seven years, Mr. Lauriston, and I've seen bodies repair from all sorts of injuries, but only if their owners allow themselves the chance to heal."

"That's what I told him," Murdo growled from the corner.

The physician chuckled, apparently not one bit

surprised by Murdo's continued presence or oddly personal interest. "You should listen to His Lordship," he told David gravely, though still with a glint of humour in his eyes.

David swallowed. He didn't want to ask the question that was burning on his tongue, but he had to, even though he already suspected the answer.

"Am I—am I well enough to return to Edinburgh, Doctor? To my legal practice?"

Murdo spoke before Dr. Logan could say anything. "Back to sitting at your desk till all hours and forgetting to eat, you mean?" he snapped. "Back to walking up and down two long flights of stairs to your rooms?"

David's face blazed with colour at the betraying intimacy of Murdo's comments.

"I don't have those rooms anymore," he said quietly.

It was an effort to remain to calm, to hide his fury at Murdo for those imprudent words. Especially when Murdo knew very well David had given up his lease. *He* was the one who had persuaded David to do it, after all. To hand back his keys and allow his belongings to be taken away to be stored at Murdo's townhouse.

"I can easily take a new lease with fewer stairs," David added into the awkward, heavy silence.

Dr. Logan cleared his throat. "Well," he said, addressing his remarks to David, "I would certainly recommend you seek rooms with as few stairs as possible. And sitting in the same chair for hours on end is not to be recommended. A gradual return to your old activities, with periods of rest and gentle exercise in between, would be best. But subject to those precautions, I would say that, yes, you are well enough to return to your practice."

Somehow David managed the mechanics of a smile in response to the doctor's verdict, though he suspected it was a wan thing.

"Good," he said. "That's good to hear."

Murdo said nothing, just glowered at them both.

"Well," the doctor said. He slapped his hands on his knees and stood up. "I'll leave you to get dressed, Mr. Lauriston, and be on my way." He quickly shrugged his coat on and packed up his bag before offering his hand to David for a hearty handshake. "Go easy on that leg," he added.

David nodded. "I will," he promised.

"I'll show you out while Mr. Lauriston dresses," Murdo said without looking at David.

For a few moments after they left, David sat there, perched on the edge of the chaise longue, his cheeks hot and his stomach in knots as he wondered what the doctor had made of this interview and the unusual interest the master of the house took in his man of business.

At last he rose and slowly dressed, though he took

his time getting ready, far from eager to resume his conversation with Murdo.

It seemed, however, that Murdo was no more eager to speak than David. He didn't come back to the sitting room at all, and when David finally ventured out, it was to discover that Murdo had asked for his horse to be saddled and was already on his way to Perth.

Murdo stayed out all day, returning only shortly before dinner.

While they dined, Murdo talked pleasantly about the various errands he'd done that day, whom he'd met and whom he'd spoken with. It was an ordinary, everyday and entirely impersonal conversation, stiff with good manners. Murdo's manners always became more pronounced when he was in a bad mood. It was one of those curiously contrary things about him.

It wasn't until they'd retired to the sitting room, taking up their usual chairs on either side of the fire, that there was a silence long enough for David to finally give voice to the matter that had been weighing on his mind all day, ever since that mortifying scene in front of Dr. Logan.

"I need to think about going back home."

He wasn't prepared for how it would feel when he actually said it. The word *home* felt like grit in his mouth, wrong and unfamiliar.

Needing to clarify, if only for himself, he added,

"To Edinburgh."

Murdo said nothing, didn't even look at David. His gaze was fixed on the rug on the floor, as though he was fascinated by the swirling pattern.

After a long silence, David added, "It's been five months."

"You're not ready," Murdo said without looking away from the rug.

"Yes I am," David replied, although the truth was, he would never be ready when being ready meant packing up and leaving Laverock House, and Murdo, for good.

"You don't take care of yourself," Murdo added in a tone that brooked no denial.

That irritated David—perhaps more so because he knew that the accusation was not without justification.

"You're worse than a bloody mother hen at times!" he snapped. "I am capable of taking care of myself, you know."

Murdo looked up at that, and his eyes flashed black fire. "Oh yes, you demonstrated that amply on Monday. You could hardly walk up the three steps to the front door when you got back from McNally's!"

"This is ridiculous," David muttered. He rose abruptly from his chair and stalked to the sideboard, suppressing an urge to curse at the twinge in his knee that accompanied the sudden movement. Lifting the whisky decanter, he sloshed a large measure of amber spirit into a glass and raised it to his lips. But before the glass could touch his mouth, Murdo was at his side, seizing his wrist. The whisky spilled on the back of his hand, immediately evaporating in the air, leaving nothing behind but coolness on his skin and the smell of alcohol in the air.

"Whisky again?" Murdo bit out. "Whenever you're confronted with something you don't like, this is your answer, isn't it?"

David stared at Murdo, stricken by the venom in his voice. The bite of Murdo's fingers on his wrist wasn't painful, but it demanded his attention.

"Other drunks talk too much," Murdo went on. "But not you. You clam up. As soon as I see you reach for the whisky, I know I'll not get another word out of you."

"I'm not a drunk," David said, hurt. He'd reduced his drinking substantially since coming to Perthshire. He thought Murdo knew that.

Wasn't Murdo right, though, a sly little voice whispered in his head, that the times he did partake were when he was upset or worried about something, just as Murdo had said? David swallowed painfully over the sudden blockage that appeared in his throat at that thought.

Murdo sighed. The anger in his gaze faded, and he let go of David's wrist. Turning away, he crossed the floor to the fireplace, where he took hold of the poker and nudged at the burnt-down logs.

After a long pause, David said quietly, "I'm not the only one who clams up about things. Every time I mention going back to Edinburgh, you shut down the conversation."

"If you're so eager to go—" Murdo began to mutter.

"I'm not," David interrupted, his voice thick with frustration. "These last few months have been the best I've—" He stopped when his voice threatened to break, and took a deep breath before continuing more calmly. "Look, we both know I have to return, sooner or later. I have to earn a living, Murdo! All those years of building up my practice… If I'm to have any kind of a chance of saving it, I have to get back to work. And you—well, you have your own plans."

Plans like marriage. Murdo had always been clear about that. He wanted what he had with David, but he wanted the trappings of respectability too.

Murdo turned to face David again and his handsome face was grim and unhappy.

"I know we have to talk about this at some point. But you don't have to make any decisions right now, do you? The fact is, your leg's *not* right yet—you've admitted as much yourself—and I have to go to London in the next day or two to take care of some things. Can we just get that out of the way first? Please?"

Murdo had been mentioning this London trip on and off for weeks now. There was business he had to take care of in the capital, he'd said, business he'd been putting off that couldn't wait much longer, though he was always vague about what that business was.

"Why is this London trip so important?"

As he expected, Murdo looked away. "It's difficult. I can't explain—not yet. Please try to understand."

David stared at him, disappointed. He said nothing, lips pressed firmly together to stop himself wheedling, and Murdo's unhappy look grew unhappier.

"Please, David, I just need you to"—he broke off with a sigh of frustration—"that is, I'm *asking* you. Will you please just wait here till I get back? I shan't be gone above a fortnight, but I'd feel happier going if I knew you would be giving yourself a little longer to recuperate." He paused, then added, "And if I knew you would be here when I return. We can talk about everything properly then."

David couldn't answer him straight away. A heavy weight in his chest was crushing all the words out of him, and he wasn't entirely sure what that weight was made of.

He managed a nod, though, and eventually, a muttered, "All right."

And then Murdo was reaching for him, and David tried to forget everything else as he lost himself in Murdo's embrace.

Chapter Three

The day after Dr. Logan's visit, David's leg was greatly improved—almost as good as it had been before he'd embarked on his ill-fated trip to McNally's. He noticed the improvement as he rose from Murdo's bed early that morning. Levering himself carefully to his feet, he waited for the inevitable pain in his knee, but instead of the slicing agony of the past few days, all that came was the lesser twinge of before.

He glanced at Murdo, thinking to share the news, but the other man was sleeping still, his face boyish and easy in slumber. David paused, admiring the familiar, handsome lines of Murdo's face, smiling at how sleep softened him. It was tempting to wake him but it was still early and the other man looked so peaceful.

Instead, David crossed the room, his bare feet nearly silent on the rug-strewn floor, to pull one of the heavy velvet drapes aside. The early morning sun streamed through the gap he'd made, illuminating the bedchamber, penetrating to the very back of the room to bathe Murdo's sleeping form in gold. Murdo shifted, murmuring a complaint, and David quietly closed the drapes again, watching as Murdo turned over and settled back to sleep.

David glanced at the clock on the mantel—it was barely six, but there was no danger of him falling back to sleep. If he returned to bed, he'd only lie there, fidgeting, and probably wake Murdo. Better to go to his own bedchamber where he could read or deal with some correspondence.

Pulling on his drawers, he headed for the door to the study that connected Murdo's bedchamber to his own. He turned the doorknob slowly so as to minimise the noise and closed it behind him just as quietly. Once, the study had been a shared dressing room for the lady and gentleman of the house, but when Murdo had first moved to Laverock House, he'd liked the morning light the room got so well that he'd decided it would be better used by him during his working hours. A serendipitous choice, it transpired. A study they both used was far more plausible as a conduit between their bedchambers than a dressing room that David could have no earthly reason to be in.

David padded past the two desks—his and Murdo's—smiling at the tidy piles of correspondence and paperwork lined up to be dealt with, and opened the door on the other side of the room, the one that led to his own bedchamber. The drapes were drawn in his bedchamber too, the bedcovers carefully mussed, and the door that gave out to the main corridor was securely locked. All of it part of his nightly routine.

He crossed to the wardrobe and drew out a set of comfortable clothes, ones that he wouldn't mind getting dirty. With his leg feeling so much better, he thought he might go fishing later, and the old-fashioned brown breeches he'd pulled out—once Murdo's—would be perfect for that, soft and worn, the matching waistcoat a loose fit on his lean form.

After tying his neckcloth in a perfunctory knot, all that remained to be done was to bring some order to his too-long hair. A dab of pomade brought it under temporary control, and, fully dressed, he threw a glance at the mirror to check his appearance, concluding with satisfaction that he didn't look *too* disreputable. He might not pass muster at Parliament House—he looked, in fact, quite the yokel in his country getup—but he would do well enough for the breakfast table at Laverock House.

Like Murdo's bedchamber, David's faced east. The early morning sunlight streamed into the room, gilding his dark-red hair with brighter flashes of copper and gold. In the instant that he turned away from the looking glass, David could have sworn he saw his brother Drew. Drew's hair had always been more fiery than his own, and those country clothes were exactly the sort of thing that Drew wore every day.

The unsettling vision made him turn back to the mirror, thinking to—what? See his brother? Of course he saw only himself, with his paler, citified complexion and darker, fox-red hair. He turned away from the glass, shaking his head.

The odd moment set him to thinking about his family, and when he took his seat behind the little writing desk at the window that looked out over Laverock House's kitchen garden, he found himself lifting a letter he'd had from his mother a few days before. He read it through once, then again, imagining her speaking the words she'd scribed in that spare way of hers.

More than half the letter was made up of questions and advice about his leg. How was his walking now? Had he used the comfrey poultice she'd recommended? He should still be using it once a week, even now that he was walking. Was there a plentiful supply of comfrey at Laverock House? And was he making sure to rub down the whole leg with her liniment every night before he retired?

His mother had been devastated to learn of David's injuries months before. And she'd felt bewildered and slighted when he'd told her that he'd be staying at Laverock House, rather than coming home to recuperate from them. He'd had to tell her that Murdo had offered him a temporary position to explain it to her in a way she could just about accept.

Well, he could write to her now and set her mind at rest on a few matters at least—the comfrey grew like wildfire in Murdo's garden, and David was positively religious about using the liniment daily—no need to admit that it was applied by his employer's hand more often than his own.

While he was dealing with correspondence, he may as well answer the other letter he'd received this week—the one from Elizabeth Chalmers.

He'd been rather surprised when Elizabeth started writing to him, but he'd grown to look forward to her letters during his recuperation. When he'd last seen her in person, she'd been running into a crowd in an attempt to flee her violent husband, Sir Alasdair Kinnell. It was David's part in her escape that had resulted in his broken leg, and a fractured skull besides. Elizabeth had got safely away, though, finding their coconspirator, Euan MacLennan, in the crowd and fleeing to London with him.

Elizabeth's first letter to David was little more than a tearstained apology about the injuries he'd sustained on her account, but there'd been one sign of defiance. The looping signature at the end of it: *Elizabeth Chalmers*, her maiden name. Her subsequent letters had shown a woman growing in confidence and happiness. And David hadn't missed the growing frequency of references to Euan. In her last few letters, Elizabeth had stopped referring to him as "Mr.

MacLennan"; he was "Euan" now. And in this latest letter, he and Elizabeth had become an obvious "we".

"We have moved again. To Blackfriars this time. It is closer to the press, which is better for Euan since he spends so much time there."

David found himself hoping that those casual *we*'s meant that Euan's love for Elizabeth was reciprocated now, or that it would be one day. They both deserved a little happiness in their lives.

He wrote steadily for an hour, first to his mother, then to Elizabeth. He was just sanding the second letter when the study door opened and Murdo appeared.

"There you are," Murdo said, the last word stretching into a yawn. He had pulled on a pair of drawers to preserve his modesty, but otherwise he was naked. His big body filled the doorframe and David allowed himself a moment to admire the breadth of the man's powerful shoulders, the soft, dark hair that covered his chest and arrowed down the flat belly he was now scratching.

"How long have you been up?" Murdo added, drawing David's attention back up to his face. A knowing smile curved his lips upwards.

David smiled back, even as his cheeks warmed at being caught out staring. "Since six. I didn't want to wake you. You were sleeping so peacefully."

"I must've been tired after last night's exertions."

Murdo grinned, and David chuckled. Their gazes met, warm with amusement and shared, secret pleasure.

Murdo leaned his head against the doorframe. "Have you had breakfast?"

David shook his head. He didn't admit that he'd wanted to wait for Murdo, but that was the truth of it. There wouldn't be too many more breakfasts together after this one. Murdo was leaving for London tomorrow. When he returned, it wouldn't be long before David had to go back to Edinburgh. All in all, they had just a handful of days together left.

"All right." Murdo yawned. "Give me a quarter of an hour to wash and dress, and we'll go down together."

"What do you plan to do today, then?" Murdo asked as he slathered his toast in butter. If David held a buttercup under Murdo's chin, he was sure the reflected light would shine like a beacon. Murdo didn't just like butter, he loved it.

"First of all, I'm going through the last batch of title deeds. They arrived from Mr. Urquhart yesterday, and I'm hoping they'll fill in the remaining gaps about the estate."

Mr. Urquhart had been Sir Hamish's solicitor. When David's letters to the man requesting the deeds to the estate had gone unanswered, David had been forced to go to Perth to see the man in person. At that stage, the reason for Urquhart's failure to respond had become clear—he was ninety, if he was a day, and, frankly, somewhat wandered. His only companion appeared to be an unmarried niece who, mortified to learn of David's errand, promised to instruct her uncle's clerk to go through all the deeds in her uncle's possession to identify those pertaining to the Laverock estate.

Due to the sheer volume of deeds held by Mr. Urquhart, not to mention the total lack of any kind of system of organisation, the task had taken a number of weeks. However, the final batch had now arrived, and David could only hope that these would help to finally make sense of the estate title once and for all, clearing up the remaining uncertainties. Having spent so long teasing out the tangled legal threads of the myriad plots that made up the estate—some inherited, some purchased, some acquired by marriage—David wanted to at least complete his research before he left Laverock House.

"Rather you than me," Murdo said.

"What about you?"

"I'm going to ride over to Howie's place this morning and take a look at his cattle. He's willing to part with a few, and I gather their yield is the envy of Perthshire."

"You're turning into quite the gentleman farmer."

"I'm learning."

"Do you want to go fishing later?" David asked.

Murdo gave a slow smile. "I'd like that."

David gave a soft laugh, even as his cheeks heated. He'd asked quite innocently, but now he remembered the last time they'd gone fishing, and what they'd got up to in their private little nook of rocks.

There hadn't been any catch that day.

Before David could answer, there was a soft knock at the door. It was Archie, the footman, bearing the morning's post on a silver tray. He placed the tray at Murdo's right hand and enquired if they wanted anything else, withdrawing when both of them shook their heads.

Murdo rifled through the pile of correspondence. "Two for you," he said, handing over two slim packets before turning his attention back to his own correspondence.

David perused his letters. He recognised the looping handwriting on one of them as that of his friend Donald Ferguson—Elizabeth's brother-in-law. Donald had been looking after some of David's cases while he was staying at Laverock House and regularly wrote to him to keep him advised as to progress and to seek David's advice.

Breaking the seal, David unfolded the letter and began to read.

My dear Lauriston,

I write to you with the gravest of news. Patrick

Chalmers is dying...

"David?"

Murdo's voice was sharp with concern, but David couldn't tear his gaze from the letter and those looping letters.

Chalmers—his mentor, the man to whom David owed his career—was dying.

Chalmers—his friend.

He thought of Elizabeth, hiding from her husband in London. She probably wouldn't get the chance to see the father she adored again, and the thought made his heart ache.

"David, what's wrong?"

"It's from Donald," David got out numbly. "Patrick Chalmers is dying, and he wants to see me."

He looked up. The stark pity in Murdo's eyes somehow made the situation feel more real, and he had to swallow against the sudden lump that appeared in his throat. "I have to go to Edinburgh."

Murdo nodded, but he added, "Are you sure you're fit to travel?"

"Yes, of course." He thought feverishly. "Do you suppose you could leave for London today instead of tomorrow? That way, I could come with you as far as Edinburgh. It would be much quicker than getting the stagecoach. Is that possible?" He frowned, thinking. "If not, perhaps Walter could take me as far as Perth, and

I'll take a coach from there—"

Murdo interrupted him. "David, slow down. We'll go today but—"

"Thank you, I—"

"*But*, will you promise me that you'll stay at the townhouse in Edinburgh while I'm in London? And…" He paused, seeming to consider for a moment before continuing. "And will you promise to make no other permanent arrangements till my return?"

David gazed at Murdo, taking in the hesitant expression and the new, unhappy lines that bracketed his mouth. This mattered to Murdo, he realised.

"All right," he said warily. "I promise."

With that vow in his pocket, Murdo seemed to minutely relax, a tension about his jaw easing enough that he managed a sad smile.

"Good," he said. Then, becoming brisk, "We'd better get packed, then."

Chapter Four

The journey to Edinburgh was very different from the one David had taken in the opposite direction five months earlier. Physically, it was a good deal more comfortable. No need for him to recline this time, his leg splinted and harnessed. This time he sat in the carriage in quite the normal way, on the bench opposite Murdo, and the most discomfort he felt was a persistent stiffness in his leg from sitting so long.

The journey was different in other ways too. Last time, he'd been journeying to an unknown place, for an unknown duration, with Murdo telling him that Laverock House would be his home for the foreseeable future. Now he was leaving that home behind. Perhaps forever.

It had occurred to him, as he packed his trunk after breakfast, how very few of his own possessions he had at Laverock House. Most of his things were being stored at Murdo's townhouse in Edinburgh. He only had a few clothes of his own—he borrowed whatever else he needed from Murdo—and some books and papers. It struck him as sad that he could pack away the last five months of his life, the richest, happiest months of all his life, he admitted to himself, into a single trunk. There was no need to leave anything behind.

A few hours ago, he'd watched from the carriage window as Laverock House grew smaller and smaller, until it disappeared altogether. And he'd thought, *I may never return here.* It had wrenched at him, that notion.

"How's the leg?"

He looked up, distracted from his thoughts by Murdo's voice. Such a distinct voice, with its deep, rich timbre and those smooth English consonants, only the barest hint of Scots in it. Murdo nodded at David's knee, and he realised that he'd been rubbing it in an absentminded way. Realised too that it ached. He made a face.

"A bit stiff," he admitted.

"You have your liniment with you," Murdo pointed out. "I'll rub it down for you, if you like."

David hesitated, torn. A leg rub sounded heavenly, but he didn't relish the thought of disrobing to any extent in the carriage. If the coachman stopped and looked in on them, what would he think?

What if, what if.

Already the world was intruding on them, making David realise how very sheltered these last months at

Laverock House had been. No need to wonder what anyone thought there. Enough space and privacy for their intimacy to be kept between the two of them, and to go unnoticed and unremarked upon.

Murdo saw his hesitancy. "Come on, let's get those breeches off. The sooner we do it, the sooner you'll be dressed again."

David weighed the risks. Their last stop had only been twenty minutes before, so there was no need for the carriage to stop anytime soon. What's more, the road had been deserted all day. There was really very little chance of him being caught in a state of undress by the coachman or anyone else. David sighed and lifted his leg, offering his booted foot to Murdo in acquiescence, smiling wryly when Murdo, grinning his triumph, grasped the heel of the boot and began to gently lever it off.

As ever, Murdo was as meticulous as any valet, careful to draw the leather sleeve away from David's tender leg in one long, smooth movement. The second boot was, as always, easier. While David undid the buttons of his breeches, Murdo moved to sit beside him, shouldering his way out of his coat and wadding it up to make a cushion of it, careless of its fine elegance.

"Put that at your back and lean against the wall," he said, handing the wadded-up coat to David. "Then lay your leg over my lap, and I'll see to you."

With another sigh, a more contented one this time, David obeyed. Just changing the position of his leg helped ease the pain, letting Murdo take the aching weight of it across his powerful thighs.

"Can you get your breeches off from there?" Murdo asked.

"Perhaps if I leave one leg on—"

Murdo made a huffing noise of frustration, cutting him off without words, and leaned over to grab hold of David's borrowed breeks and tug at them, forcing David to arch his hips off the seat. A moment later, Murdo had drawn them off altogether and tossed them unceremoniously onto the opposite bench. The next moment he was rolling down the stocking on David's right leg and peeling that off too.

David watched, unprotesting now, as his injured limb, pale and somewhat wasted still, was laid bare. Despite regular exercise, his right leg remained slightly thinner than the left. The knee looked wrong to David too, a bit off centre somehow. He made a face, not liking the sight of his weakness. It wasn't just how it looked. It was the physical reminder of everything he couldn't do. Walk, climb, run. The things he'd always loved and, until now, had taken for granted. Abilities he may never fully recover.

"What's wrong?" Murdo asked. He missed nothing, damn him.

"I hate the look of it," David said shortly. "It's

ugly."

Murdo's brows drew together in a puzzled expression. He turned his head to the offending limb, caressing the length of it with his hands while David watched. Murdo had strong, capable hands that could rub the pain in David's leg away, gentle hands that could wring such sharp pleasure from David's body that he couldn't stop himself crying out from it.

David watched, mesmerised, as Murdo went through the now-familiar motions of opening the liniment jar, dipping his fingers in to get a bit of the dense, waxy stuff, then rubbing it between his hands, releasing a scent that David would associate forever with soothing comfort and relief. And then Murdo's hands were on David, slowly sweeping up the length of his thigh, his thumbs digging into the wasted, perennially tired muscles, the blunt heels of his hands kneading and working over the damaged architecture of David's injured limb.

David closed his eyes, giving himself over to the singular pleasure of pain relief, letting himself have this, take this. This freely offered gift.

"It's not ugly," Murdo murmured. "Nothing about you could ever be ugly to me."

His voice was soft and deep, as free from laughter as David had ever heard it, and David's heart clenched in the cage of his chest to detect the sincerity in it. He swallowed, embarrassed to realise that Murdo had probably seen the bob of his throat and correctly read its meaning.

This vulnerability seemed to grow deeper each day, in direct proportion to the depth of his feelings. The two were linked, quite inextricably, his affection for Murdo exposing him in ways that horrified him. The protective barriers he'd spent a lifetime building up felt like they were crumbling away in the face of emotions he was helpless to deny. There would be no protection left to him when this ended.

And the end was coming.

The black descent that came after the end would be upon him very soon. He'd been through it once before, but this time it would be much, much worse.

The soothing hands on his leg stilled, and when David opened his eyes, it was to see Murdo watching him with an expression caught somewhere between sadness and concern. David's chest ached, and all he could think to do to ease the feeling was to look away. He busied himself with sitting up, swinging his legs off Murdo's lap and making a show of searching the floor of the carriage.

"Where on earth's my stocking?" he said, amazed to hear how prosaic he sounded.

He found it at last, keeping his gaze averted from Murdo as he rolled the fine-knit material over his calf, his skin still faintly sticky from the liniment, then stretched across the carriage to fetch his crumpled breeches from the opposite bench.

"David—"

Murdo's hand on his shoulder pulled him back. He didn't resist, allowing Murdo to draw him back down onto the bench, though he kept his gaze on his own hands and the soft brown material bunched between his fingers.

"What's wrong?"

David just sat there. What could he say? That their affection for one another, so obvious during that tender moment a minute ago—*"Nothing about you could ever be ugly to me."*—made David feel…unsafe? Worse, that he knew now he'd never be safe again, that he had lost the safety of his splendid isolation the moment Murdo Balfour had walked back into his life six months before?

That every day made him more vulnerable? That the thought of their parting…

"It's nothing," he lied. "I'm just—" He broke off.

"Is it about Chalmers?"

Guilt welled at Murdo's assumption. How could he be thinking of himself when the only reason he was in this carriage was to see Chalmers one last time before he died?

He swallowed. "Donald's letter said he hasn't long now."

"Don't worry," Murdo replied. "We'll get you there on time."

The sudden reality of his friend's imminent death struck David at that moment like a great wave. It swamped his heart with a powerful crash, then ebbed away, leaving behind a rocky debris of regret and grief that clawed at him.

Life was very fragile.

"I should go and see my family soon," David said, surprising himself.

"You miss them," Murdo said, and it wasn't a question.

"Yes. They are good people." Being with them nourished something in him, doing him as much good as the wholesome broth his mother made.

Murdo smiled. "Well, you had to get all that virtue from somewhere."

David gave a weak laugh. "Are you teasing me again? I know you think I'm sanctimonious at times."

Murdo laughed too, but it was a soft, affectionate chuckle, no teasing in it.

David pulled on the breeches then. He buttoned them up and straightened his clothes, and when he was done, he sat back down next to Murdo, enjoying the warmth of the other man's leg against his own.

After a while, Murdo said, "I thought that you and your father weren't on the best of terms? You told me he hit you when he found you with your friend that time."

He was referring to the time David's father had

come upon him kissing Will Lennox when David was sixteen, a discovery that had prompted David's gentle father to strike David for the first and only time in his life.

David shook his head. "We are not on bad terms. We don't speak of it at all—my father's an elder of the Kirk and he worries for my soul, but he believes that if I don't act on my desires, God won't punish me, so he is able to live with it, that way."

"I take it from that, that you give him no reason to believe you act on your desires?"

"No, I never would. I don't wish to give him any more reason to worry. He's suffered enough sleepless nights over me."

Murdo laughed shortly. "God, we couldn't be more different. Over the years I've taken great pleasure in thumbing my nose at my father. I still do."

David stilled. Murdo never spoke about his father. Not voluntarily.

After a long pause, David said with studied casualness, "He knows you prefer men?"

Murdo gave one of his mirthless huffs of laughter. "My father knows everything about everyone, and—as he has reminded me all my life—knowledge is power. He uses his knowledge to persuade people to act as he wishes them to."

His tone was bitter, revealing.

"Has he used knowledge about you to compel you

to act as he wishes?"

Murdo stared at the empty bench opposite them, his expression grim.

"All my life—or tried to, at least. He was probably rubbing his hands together in glee when he found out about my preference for men—such a good bit of blackmail material."

"But wouldn't a son with such preferences reflect poorly on him?" David asked, half-appalled, half-curious. "Surely he has a vested interest in keeping it quiet?"

"You would think so, wouldn't you? But my father is far more devious than you can possibly imagine. When I pointed out that a sodomite for a son would do his political career no favours—I was seventeen at the time, I believe—he replied that he would never allow my disgrace to be made public. Rather than allow my proclivities to pose a threat to the honour of the family name, he would admit me to an asylum—to be cured, you understand."

David stared, appalled. "Perhaps he was worried for you and thought the fear of committal would keep you on the straight and narrow?"

Again, Murdo laughed, a hateful sound, harsh and contemptuous. "Oh no, he doesn't mind about my preferences, you see. Everything serves a purpose in my father's world. Once we had reached our understanding—my compliance in exchange for his tolerance—he was quick to put me to use. Before long I was tasked with befriending a man he wanted some information on. Someone with the same…interests. In fact—" He paled noticeably and broke off, exhaling sharply. "Never mind."

David had never seen Murdo so shaken. Carefully, he touched his lover's knee, stroking gently with his thumb. "Tell me."

To David's alarm, Murdo dropped his head into his hands and let out a shuddering sigh. He stayed like that for a long time. Eventually, in a thin voice, he said, "Do you remember me telling you about the first time I was buggered?"

Buggered. David balked at the ugly word, at the wrongness of it being applied to Murdo. It took him a few moments to think back to another conversation, months before.

"I remember. You said there were two men," David said slowly. "And that they were rough with you." Even as he spoke, a kind of realisation began to dawn, and nausea swirled in his gut. "Please tell me that had nothing to do with your father."

Murdo didn't deny it. "The one my father had asked me to befriend was called Gilliam," he said flatly. "Somehow, he found out who I really was. I'd arranged to meet him at a house in the country for the weekend, and they—he and his friend—well, they really let me have it. Threw me in a carriage once they were done, and sent me home as a message to my father."

Somehow, David managed to keep the hand on Murdo's knee stroking gently, soothingly, even as a wild animal clawed in his chest to get out. To get out and find this Gilliam and his friend. And Murdo's father.

Murdo lifted his head out of his hands, though he still didn't look at David. "It was fifteen years ago," he said disgustedly. "Yet even now, it affects me like this."

"Of course it does," David protested gently. "It would affect anyone like this." Under his fingers, he could feel Murdo's tension. The thrum of it was almost like a vibration beneath his fingers, and he couldn't make his mind up whether all that nervous energy was trying to reject David's compassion or clamouring for it. Certainly Murdo didn't reach for him. He rested his elbows on his thighs and held his hands in front of his face, loosely clasped. He'd made a cage of himself, with David on the outside. David's hand on Murdo's knee was the only connection between them, but since Murdo let it rest there, David reasoned he must want it to stay.

"My father made sure Gilliam paid for that insult later, but even so, that was the episode that made me realise just how dispensible I was to him. After that, I decided I had to get out from under his thumb. And since he held the purse strings, the only way to do it was to become financially independent."

"How old were you when this happened?"

The story was pouring out of him now, no hesitation in the answer that followed.

"Almost twenty. I was done with Oxford by then, ready for something new. So I set about learning finance and trade. My Uncle Gideon was only too pleased to help me—he detests my father—and I had the benefit of aristocratic connections galore, of course, which Gideon liked.

"I worked hard, but I'm under no illusions. The thing that really made me successful was that I took advantage of all the privileges of my standing. I used my name to open doors and bring others with me. I built and built my fortune till I was satisfied I'd never need the old man again. Then I kept building it. I wanted an estate of my own, one that my father had no connection to. I wanted to be able to buy and sell him." Murdo glanced at David over one hunched shoulder, revealing a glimmer of vulnerability. "I've spent the last fifteen years plotting to get away from him. It's what this trip to London is all about."

David opened his mouth to ask what he meant by that—what Murdo planned to do in London—but when he saw the distraught look on Murdo's face, he stopped himself. Now was not the time to plague Murdo with questions David already knew he was reluctant to answer. Instead, he leaned in, pressing his side against Murdo's, his hand still resting on the other man's knee, musing over what Murdo had just told him.

"I'm so sorry that happened to you," David murmured at last, turning his head to press a kiss to Murdo's neck. The scent of bitter orange from Murdo's hair pomade filled his nostrils, familiar and oddly comforting.

"No need for you to be sorry."

"I know, but I'm sorry anyway. Sorry I wasn't there to stop it. I wish I could make it right."

"So very like you to want to put things right," Murdo murmured. He turned his head till their eyes met, and his dark gaze was warm with affection. His lips sought David's, and their mouths moved together in a consoling kiss that had nothing to do with passion.

"David," he said, when they broke apart. "David."

He said David's name like it meant something all on its own.

Like a vow.

Like a promise.

Chapter Five

It was past five o'clock when they reached Murdo's Queen Street townhouse. Their arrival flustered the housekeeper. She hadn't expected Murdo till the following day, and now she trailed them to the drawing room, apologising profusely that the bedchambers weren't ready yet. His Lordship's was being aired, she said, and she hadn't realised that Mr. Lauriston would be joining him.

Although that last observation was offered by way of apologetic excuse, David felt an immediate pang of anxiety. Did she think it odd he was here, and unannounced no less?

Murdo, of course, was unconcerned. He brushed the housekeeper's apologies aside with a careless smile, saying that some tea and scones would occupy them very well while their chambers were made up, if she'd be good enough to see to it.

David watched as she left the room, an upright, starched little woman, nodding sharply at the footman who held the door open for her, as correct as any sergeant major.

David wondered about the footman too. Although the man's expression was impassive now, David fancied he'd seen a flicker of curiosity there when they had entered the room. Or perhaps he was being ridiculous.

That was entirely possible. He'd been feeling conspicuous all day—as though he had a sign round his neck that declared him to be Lord Murdo Balfour's lover. It was, after all, the first time they'd gone anywhere together since they'd begun to regularly share a bed. Suddenly, David found himself wondering what expression he wore when he looked at Murdo, whether he was standing too close to him, whether the casual little touches that Murdo bestowed on him—his hand on David's arm, or at the small of his back—were unexceptional or entirely betraying.

"I've been dying to kiss you," Murdo said now, interrupting David's train of thought. Although they were alone and the door was firmly closed, David still felt a bolt of panic. His gaze flickered to the only other possible threat—the window—and he stepped back from Murdo's advance.

"Not here," he said. "The drapes are wide open."

Murdo just smiled. "We're on the second floor, and there are no houses opposite. No one can see."

"Nevertheless"—David broke off, looking around, a shiver of unease running through him—"anyone could walk in."

Murdo frowned. "No one walks in on me in my own house. My servants know to knock."

David didn't feel reassured. He moved across the room, his cane tapping on the polished parquet floor, to investigate just how private the window was.

It was, of course, as Murdo had said—and as David already *knew*—entirely private. Just the street below them and, opposite, the broad, green stretch of square after square of private gardens. Not that they looked green right now. Already, it was dusk, and the world was suffused in the half-grey light that prevailed just before full darkness fell. At this time of day, the gardens looked shadowy and vaguely threatening.

Fenced round and locked up tight, these gardens were for the exclusive use of the proprietors of the houses that overlooked them. For some, it was a place to walk and sit, safe from the filth and squalor of the inconvenient poor of the city. There were others, though, who never stepped foot inside the gardens. For them, the gardens were a guarantee of privacy, a protection from anyone building more houses on their doorstep.

If you had enough money, you could protect yourself from most things. You could surround yourself with broad, green stretches.

Even then, though, sooner or later, you had to face the world.

Today David had left the broad, green stretches of

Laverock House behind him. It felt different here. Murdo might ignore his servants, but David hadn't missed their silent, careful interest. They would be speaking about him below stairs now, he was quite sure. The man who had been brought here, injured, months before. The man whose bedside the master had barely left for weeks, and who'd then gone with the master to his new estate in Perthshire.

"They must be wondering about me," David murmured, turning to meet Murdo's frowning gaze. "Your servants, I mean."

"Quite apart from the fact that it's none of their business, they know who you are. You were here before, after all."

"That was different. I was injured. I needed help. Now I'm perfectly able to manage on my own." David paused before adding, "Perhaps I shouldn't stay on when you go to London tomorrow. I could easily take a room at an inn instead."

"For God's sake!" Murdo exclaimed. He stared at David, all impatience and disbelief, then sighed. "You're in one of your moods, I see. Imagining all sorts of nonsense." He pinched the bridge of his nose before continuing more calmly. "It's perfectly commonplace for gentlemen to put their friends up in their homes, David. Sometimes for months at a time."

David pressed his lips together, resenting the implication that he was being absurd. "That may be the case for men who're social equals, but we're *not* equals."

Murdo sent him another incredulous look, black eyebrows raised. "Are you of all people suggesting you're my inferior?"

"Of course not," David replied, irritated now. "But that doesn't mean I don't see how other people view us. I don't want you to be exposed to rumour—not any more than I want to be exposed to it. Our friendship is not without risk, Murdo, you *know* that. We have to take reasonable precautions not to draw suspicion."

Murdo stared at him for a long moment. "I honestly don't understand where this has come from," he said. "What's prompted all these worries? You gave no hint of any of these concerns in the carriage on the way here."

David sighed and turned to look out of the window again. Already the sky had darkened further. Soon it would be fully night.

"It's just—coming here, back to Edinburgh, seeing the servants' reaction to me arriving with you—"

"What reaction?" Murdo asked, sounding genuinely bewildered.

"Just because you didn't notice it, doesn't mean there wasn't one," David said wearily.

Murdo was silent for a moment; then he said, "It's not just that, though, is it?" He stepped closer and laid his hand on David's shoulder, and the comfort of that touch was both reassuring and unbearable, promising far too much, making David want things he couldn't have.

"No," David admitted, staring out at the darkening sky. "It isn't just that. It's leaving Laverock House—I've been so happy there, and now it's coming to an end, and—"

"David—"

"—and as much as I wish I didn't have to go back to my old life, I *do* have to."

Silence.

Finally, David turned round again, and he saw that Murdo's eyes held sadness. They glimmered, ink black in the candlelight, till he veiled the emotion in them with a down sweep of his thick lashes.

"It needn't be over," Murdo murmured. "*I* don't want it to be—you must know how much I care for you..." His lashes lifted, and David met that dark—now beloved—gaze again. *Did* he know how much Murdo cared for him?

This thing between them was more than friendship, more than desire too. More than he could bring himself to speak aloud. Speaking it would give it a name, and once it had a name, he was lost. The black descent was going to be bad enough without that.

David closed his eyes against the burning emotion in Murdo's gaze. When he opened them again, he had himself a little more under control.

"I'm going out," he said. "I want to find out from

Donald how things stand before I go up to see Chalmers."

Murdo searched his face for a moment. "All right," he sighed. "Go and do what you need to. We'll talk about this later."

Donald and Catherine Ferguson didn't live too far from Murdo's house, but while he had a whole townhouse to himself, they occupied only the upper half of a similarly sized, if slightly less grand property. When David called on them at half past six, they were just about to sit down to dinner, and Donald insisted he join them.

"Come on," he said, leading the way upstairs. "There's plenty of mutton to go round, and Catherine will be pleased to see you."

"There's no need to feed me," David protested, even as he followed Donald upstairs.

"Don't be silly," Donald said good-naturedly. "As though we'd think of eating while you watch."

Their home was cosy and comfortable looking, David thought as he followed Donald through the hallway and into the dining room. With its hotchpotch of rugs and framed needlepoint pictures—Catherine's, David presumed—on the walls, it was far less elegant than Murdo's house, but far less intimidating too.

Catherine rose from the table when they entered the small dining room. She smiled at David, but it was a wan smile and there were lines of strain about her eyes.

"I'm so glad you're here, Mr. Lauriston," she said as he bowed over her hand. "Father so particularly wants to see you. He's mentioned it to me the last several times I've visited him."

Chalmers was still hanging on, then. Thank God for that.

"I'm equally anxious to see him."

"Let's have something to eat while we talk," she suggested.

As they settled themselves at the table, David took in the changes that the last few months had wrought on his friends. Catherine—until now, a round and vivacious girl—was noticeably thinner, her manner much more subdued than the girl he remembered. She served only a very small portion of food onto her own plate and pushed what was there around for the most part, eating little. Was she too anxious about her father to eat, David wondered?

Donald was changed too. Always the most jolly of men, he looked suddenly careworn, his forehead etched with deep furrows from frowning.

"Forgive my bluntness," David said when the inevitable small talk had been disposed of, "but—how is your father?"

Catherine and Donald exchanged a look, then Donald said, "He does not have long left, David. It will be a matter of days."

Catherine flinched at that, though she didn't disagree.

David paused. "Then I should like to see him as soon as I can. Would this evening be possible?"

Catherine pressed her lips together unhappily. "I'm afraid Mama won't have visitors in the evening. She says Father's too tired."

"Surely, given the circumstances—" David began carefully.

Donald interrupted, his tone flat. "Your best bet is tomorrow morning. She won't refuse you then, not when he's specifically asked for you. Otherwise, I suspect she'd take great delight in sending you away— She never liked you, you know."

"Donald—" Catherine protested weakly.

"Well, it's true!" he retorted. He turned to David again. "She was convinced you had designs on Elizabeth, even though it was plain as day that you weren't the least bit interested. And, of course, she blames you for Elizabeth running away."

Catherine sighed. "I know it's not satisfactory, Mr. Lauriston. But you're probably better visiting in the morning anyway. Father takes a sleeping draught every evening, and once he's had it, he becomes a little disorientated."

That was all very well, David thought, provided Chalmers was still around tomorrow morning. But he nodded his agreement and allowed Catherine to change the subject.

As soon as the meal was over, Catherine excused herself, pleading tiredness.

"Is Catherine all right?" David asked Donald once she had left the room. Donald was busy getting some whisky out of the sideboard, but at David's question, he paused, staring down at the decanter in his hands.

"Not really," he said simply. "She suffered a miscarriage a few weeks ago. On top of everything else, it was pretty unbearable for her."

"Oh God, I'm so sorry."

Donald looked up and gave a sad half smile. "The doctor sees no reason to worry she won't conceive again. It's just—she's still very dejected about it. She tries to hide it when people are around, but when we're alone, she's inconsolable. And it's not just the baby. She was frantic about Lizzie when she ran off, and now there's her father, dying. Catherine adores him. All the girls do." He sighed and set the whisky down on the table, fetching two glasses before he settled back in his chair and poured them both a large measure.

"She hasn't been herself for weeks," he continued gruffly. "I've been working here as much as I can, so I can keep an eye on her. I don't like her being too much alone. It makes her melancholy."

"I'm so sorry," David said again. "Catherine's always been such a merry girl."

Donald sighed again, a heavy, careworn sound.

"And I've been so preoccupied with work."

David felt an immediate stab of guilt. Donald had taken a raft of cases off David's hands when David had gone to Perthshire with Murdo to recuperate from his accident. Donald had dealt too with all the trustees' duties for the trust Chalmers had put in place to provide for Elizabeth, even though, as his cotrustee, David should have borne an equal share of the responsibility.

"I'm sorry, Donald," he said now. "I've taken you for granted. You'll have to let me know what I can do to rectify matters."

"Don't be silly." Donald pasted on a ramshackle smile. "It's not as though I didn't get paid for dealing with your cases. I'm not that much of a martyr!"

"Even so. You're overworked and worried about Catherine. We'll work something out. I need to start thinking about my own future in any event." He paused, then added, "And what about Elizabeth?"

Donald shrugged. "It's still too risky for her to return to Scotland—we're sure Kinnell's had Chalmers's house watched. Ours too, probably." He rubbed a weary hand over his eyes. "The fact is, she'll never see her father again, and that's difficult for everyone. Catherine's been especially upset by it, particularly when her mother uses it as an excuse to malign Lizzie."

David could just imagine. Elizabeth's mother

would have detested the scandal Elizabeth had caused.

After a pause, David asked, "Do you know why Chalmers wants to see me?"

"Well, Lord knows he's fond of you—boasts about your achievements like you're his own flesh and blood." Donald paused. "It's possible he wishes only to say good-bye, but I can't help thinking there's more to it. I know he's worried about Elizabeth too. I've tried to get him to talk to me, but…" He trailed away helplessly.

"I'll go to him first thing tomorrow."

Donald lifted his glass and said, "Let's pray he lasts another night."

Chapter Six

David was just about to leave the townhouse the next morning when Murdo entered the hallway behind him.

"You forgot something."

David turned his head to be confronted by the ebony-and-silver cane and an expression on Murdo's face that dared David to defy him.

"Chalmers's house is less than ten minutes away," David protested, but Murdo just kept holding out the cane.

"You should take it with you whenever you go out." His expression softened at whatever look he saw on David's face, and he added more gently, "For now."

David sighed, but he took the cane, though somewhat ungraciously.

"Fine," he huffed and turned to the door again.

"Make sure you're back for dinner," Murdo said in an imperious tone he sometimes used that got on David's nerves.

David turned back to look at him, irritated. "Must

you order me around like that?" he demanded. "I'm not one of your footmen, and anyway, dinner's eight hours away."

Murdo's jaw was set and belligerent. "I'm not ordering you around, merely asking you to ensure you are back sooner rather than later. After all, I'm setting off for London first thing tomorrow morning."

And in that moment, David saw what this was really about.

"I promise I'll be back," he said. "We'll have tonight, Murdo."

Murdo's gaze slid away, his cheeks pinkening slightly as he turned aside. "All right, I'll see you later then."

David was still half smiling over their exchange as he left the townhouse, despite the fact that he hated the cane and that he was dreading what he would find when he reached Chalmers's house.

He wasn't long out the door, though, before he wished he'd argued his point about the cane a bit harder. He preferred not to use it when he didn't need to, and for such a short walk it seemed ridiculous. He hated the tapping noise the silver tip made when it struck the cobbles under his feet, a constant reminder of his disability, as if the ache in his hip and knee wasn't enough.

When he arrived at Chalmers's house, though, all thoughts of his own troubles and petty concerns fled. It hadn't occurred to him that there would be any outward sign of the man who lay dying inside, but of course there was. The pavement and road in front of his friend's house was strewn with a thick layer of straw to muffle the sounds of passing carriages and horses and the footsteps of pedestrians. It was an outward sign of terrible sickness. Of imminent death. And for the first time, David felt the truth of it—Chalmers really was dying.

He approached the front door slowly, staring at its glossy exterior for a moment before raising his hand to knock. The maidservant who answered was quiet and subdued, keeping her gaze downcast as she stood aside to let David pass.

Inside, the house was as silent as the muffled cobbles outside. David was shown into the drawing room, where he took a seat on a stiff horsehair sofa, balancing his cane beside him. While he waited, he became fascinated by the out-of-time ticking of the two clocks in the room, the deep-toned longcase in the corner and the chirpy ormolu on the mantel. The smaller one ticked an instant after the larger one so that it seemed they kept two times, two sets of twenty-four hours, one running a fraction of a second ahead of the other.

After a while, the door opened and a woman entered. David's first thought was how relieved he was it wasn't Mrs. Chalmers, with whom he'd dreaded making stilted conversation. The woman who came in was younger than Mrs. Chalmers, and she was dressed in a sober grey gown, with a white apron and a white lace cap that covered her hair so thoroughly David couldn't have said what colour it was.

"Mr. Lauriston," she said, approaching him. Her voice was low and pleasant.

He stood up quickly, making the cane clatter to the floor. The woman had reached him now, and she bent to pick it up at the same moment David did, causing them to bump heads.

"Oh, that was clumsy of me. I do beg your pardon," David said.

"Not at all." She laughed, handing the cane over. "My fault entirely. It's second nature to me to pick things up after people, I'm afraid. I'm Mrs. Jessop, Mr. Chalmers's nurse."

David bowed. "I'm pleased to make your acquaintance, ma'am."

"Mr. Chalmers will be pleased to see you, sir. He's been asking after you for the last few days. Since Mr. Ferguson said he'd written to ask you to come."

"How is he?"

Mrs. Jessop's expression remained serene, but her pale gaze softened with sad sympathy. "Not well, sir. I'm afraid it will not be long now."

"How long do you think?"

She shook her head. "Impossible to say for certain, but no more than a few days, I would think. Every morning he wakes is a blessing now."

The solid lump of grief in David's throat felt like it was choking him. Mrs. Jessop spared his pride by turning away.

"Come," she said. "I'll take you to him."

Somehow, David shambled himself back together again and followed her out into the hall. They ascended the broad, winding staircase together, David's eyes fixed on the nurse's dove-grey skirts.

She led him to one of the bedchambers and knocked softly at the door before opening it a crack. "Mr. Chalmers, I have someone to see you."

"Come in," said a weak, listless voice, barely recognisable to David. Mrs. Jessop opened the door all the way, stepping to one side to allow David to precede her.

The man who lay against the white pillows in Chalmers's bed was a stranger. The last time David had seen his friend, he'd looked unwell—thinner and frailer—but this was something else altogether. Now he was shrunk to skin and bones, and his face was gaunt. In the morning light, his sallow skin had a papery look, and his once twinkling eyes were dull and sunken.

When his gaze alighted on David, though, that terrible death mask somehow cracked for a moment and David saw a glimpse of his old friend.

"David—"

Chalmers began struggling—and failing—to raise himself up on one elbow. David stepped forward to help, wondering how to do so, but before he could formulate a plan, Mrs. Jessop was at Chalmers's side, doing something discreet and easy looking with a pile of pillows. Half a minute later, Chalmers was sitting up, in a fashion, reclining against a great snowy bolster the nurse had made for him.

"There now," she said. "I'll leave you, but I'll bring some tea up in a little while, shall I?" She didn't wait for an answer but smoothly glided away, closing the door behind her with a tiny click.

"My friend," David said softly, walking forward. "It's good to see you."

"And you, lad." Chalmers's thin voice was a mere whisper, but somehow he imbued the words he uttered with a rich mix of emotions, relief and pleasure and sorrow all at once.

David sat himself down in the single empty chair beside the bed. Chalmers raised his right hand in a weak greeting, and David took it between both of his own. Shocked by how cold and brittle it felt, he chafed it gently between his fingers. When he looked at Chalmers's face again, he was horrified to feel tears leap into his eyes.

Ducking his head, he muttered, "I'm sorry."

But Chalmers merely gave a wheezy chuckle. "Don't be. I'm gratified to—to merit tears."

David managed a faint chuckle of his own at that typically Chalmers comment, though it was a sad effort, in truth.

"I'm glad you got here in time, lad. Before I—"

"Don't—"

"—before I die," Chalmers continued with gentle emphasis, adding with a sad smile, "It won't be long now, lad." He fell silent then, for so long that David wondered if he had it in him to talk anymore.

"Do you have something you want to tell me?" David prompted after a while. "Or something to ask of me? You know I will do whatever is in my power."

"I know," Chalmers breathed. "You have been a good friend to me. And yes, I have something to—ask."

"Name it."

"I'll come to it. First, have you seen Kitty and Donald?"

David nodded. "Last night, I dined with them."

"Then you'll know how"—he seemed to search for words, and perhaps also for breath—"how delicate Kitty is."

David paused, unsure how much to say. In the end, he settled for, "Kitty'll be all right. Donald will take care of her. You know that, don't you?"

Chalmers nodded. "Donald's a good lad." He closed his eyes, his brow furrowing as though he was in pain, while his thin chest rose and fell with his shaky breaths.

When he opened his eyes again, he said sadly, "Poor Kitty. She was always—always my sunny girl."

David gazed at the other man earnestly. "And she will be again. She's had a hard time of it, but she'll come round, with Donald's help. She's strong, and no woman could want a more attentive husband."

A faint nod at that and a matching smile, happy and melancholy all at once. "They are happy together. A true love match. That's—" He broke off, closing his eyes and tensing again. David raised himself from his chair and leaned over the other man, concerned but not knowing what to do.

After a minute, Chalmers opened his eyes and gestured shakily at the jug on his nightstand. David carefully poured him a cup of what looked like plain water and held it to Chalmers's lips, slipping his arm around the other man's shoulders to support him while he drank. He could feel Chalmers's shoulder blades through his nightshirt, sharp and frail, and the weight of him was puny on David's arm. He was like a husk, dried out and ready to blow away with the winds.

Once Chalmers had drunk his fill and rested for a minute, he began to talk again.

"My Kitty married a man she loves, thank God. It's the only reason to marry, lad."

David watched his friend. Chalmers knew better than anyone how often people married for reasons other than love. His own marriage was a cold affair. What was more, Elizabeth, his oldest and favourite daughter, had married Sir Alasdair Kinnell after being disappointed in love by David himself. David, guilty over his clumsy rejection of her, had been relieved to hear of the marriage, glad that she'd married so well. It was only later that he learned how Kinnell was abusing her.

"I did not marry for love," Chalmers said. "Margaret was the daughter of a senior man at the bar. Four years older than I. Her father let it be known she had a good dowry, and that he'd give my career a leg up." He closed his eyes. "I was ambitious back then."

David was not surprised to hear that Chalmers's marriage had been devoid of any tender feelings, even at the beginning. Chalmers's wife was a proud, haughty woman. She'd shown no affection and little respect for her husband in all the time David had known Chalmers, and she didn't bother to hide her contempt for anyone he invited into their home whom she considered to be inferior.

"I would not change anything now," Chalmers continued. "I have four wonderful girls who I love more than life. But the truth is, our marriage was never a happy one. She was always cold." He closed his eyes again, breathing against another wave of pain. For a while he was silent, then he added, "And perhaps I was too. We were never more than strangers who lived in the same house."

David couldn't help but contrast the bleak picture Chalmers presented with his own parents' quiet contentment. They had never had the money or position enjoyed by Chalmers and his wife, but they had something else far more valuable, a deep love for one another that had survived a hundred trials—lost babies and bad harvests and severe winters. No matter how bad things had ever been for them, they always had each other to lean on.

"It must have been difficult," David murmured, "to live like that. Like strangers."

"I didn't realise how much, till I met someone I truly cared for," Chalmers confessed, his voice raw with emotion. He paused before adding, "I did not set out to do it. She was a client—a widow. We became friends first. Then, much later, lovers."

David was shocked. He'd never even guessed at this. Chalmers had given no hint of it before. "Does she know about this?" he asked. "Your illness, I mean?"

Chalmers shook his head. He closed his eyes, and his throat bobbed as he swallowed. Eventually, he said, "She passed away three years ago."

"Ah God, Chalmers, I'm sorry."

"At the time, it was terrible. There was no one I could speak to about her. She was the love of my life, and I had to act as though she had never existed. As though my heart had not been destroyed."

David's heart squeezed at that painful confession. "What was her name?"

"Mary. Mary Cunningham."

"I'm glad that you—that you found some happiness with her." The words came out rather stiltedly, but they were sincerely meant, and somehow David knew Chalmers understood that.

"And I'm glad I can speak of her to someone. For all this time, it has felt as though I've been denying her very existence. Denying that I loved her." He paused. "Love should not be denied."

"She'd have understood," David replied, believing it.

Chalmers didn't answer that right away, but at last he said quietly, "I don't know about that. She died alone. After she took ill, I hired a nurse for her, since I couldn't be with her all the time. It happened after I left her one evening so I could attend a dinner party Margaret had arranged." He closed his eyes and his voice shook with regret as he continued. "She died in the early hours of the morning. I was not with her, and I should have been. I can never get that chance back again—to be there for her when she passed. I was too busy slinking back here to dine with some bore Margaret wanted me to charm."

The agony on Chalmers's face was palpable. This was a soul-deep pain, far worse in its way than the physical pain the man now endured.

"Do you still think she'd have understood, lad?" Chalmers whispered.

David couldn't deny that Chalmers's confession altered his view. He found himself imagining Murdo leaving his side to perform an obligation to some hypothetical future wife and was surprised at how painful he found the mere thought. Not that he intended to find himself in such a position. He'd decided long ago that he would break off with Murdo as and when a potential wife appeared on the scene.

"But that is not even my greatest regret," Chalmers continued in a pained voice.

"What is then?"

"That I did not tell Mary I loved her till she was too ill to understand the words."

Chalmers's face was twisted into an expression of self-loathing, and David's heart ached for his friend. "I'll wager she knew," he whispered. But Chalmers just shook his head.

"Words have power," he said. "I held my confession back to punish myself for my infidelity. But when Mary lay dying, I realised I had punished her too. Saying the words was"—a shaking breath—"it was far more powerful than I realised it would be. But without Mary to hear those words, they were stillborn. Sometimes things must be said." He closed his eyes. "And they must be heard too."

Chalmers sank back into his pillows, exhausted

after that relatively lengthy exchange, and fell into a light, fitful slumber.

Mrs. Jessop popped her head in again while he dozed. She carried a tea tray, which she set down on the sideboard. She poured some tea for David, dosing his cup with both milk and sugar before passing it to him. It wasn't at all how he liked it—but he drank it down gratefully while she checked on Chalmers. There was a cup for Chalmers too, though not of tea, in his case. Mrs. Jessop sat it on the nightstand beside his bed, ready for when he woke. Then she tiptoed from the room again.

At length, Chalmers stirred. He grimaced, almost comically, when David pointed out the draught beside his head, though he let David help him sit up straighter, the better to drink it down.

David held the cup to Chalmers's lips and the older man accepted most of the contents before leaning back against his pillows again.

"So, I have a favour to ask you, David."

"Name it."

"It is to do with Elizabeth."

David didn't pause. "I guessed as much."

Another wait while Chalmers gathered his strength again. David was coming to learn his dying friend's rhythms, and they were heartbreakingly slow.

"I had a letter last week from Charles Carr, my brother-in-law. He is the solicitor administering

Elizabeth's trust."

"Yes, I remember." Although David was one of Elizabeth's trustees, so far he'd had no need to perform any duties since Donald had taken that burden on his shoulders after David's accident. "Is there a problem?"

"It's Kinnell. He's been to Charles's office. He was asking questions about Elizabeth."

David stared helplessly at his friend, trying not to betray how profoundly this news, that Elizabeth's husband was so close to her, scared him. He'd experienced firsthand what Kinnell was capable of when he had his wife in his sights.

"Charles doesn't think it means Kinnell knows about the trust, or even that she's in London," Chalmers continued. "Kinnell may have just gone to see him on the off chance—he knows Charles is family—but equally, he could have been watching Charles's offices."

Charles's office, where Elizabeth went to collect her trust income every month.

David searched for something reassuring to say, but before he could come up with anything, Chalmers spoke again.

"I want you to move the business of administering the trust to another solicitor—preferably in another city altogether, if Elizabeth can be prevailed upon to leave London. Only one of the trustees can deal with this." He paused and sent David a regretful look.

"David—I know it isn't fair to ask you, but I can't ask Donald. Not with Kitty as she is."

"Is that all?" David asked. "No need to apologise, old friend. Consider it done."

"I shouldn't be asking you," Chalmers replied unhappily. "I know you're not fully recovered."

"Well, I don't need to be for this. It so happens that Lord Murdo leaves for London tomorrow, and I'm sure he'll be willing to take me with him in his carriage, so I'll travel like a king and be in the capital within the week." He paused briefly. "And I'll do what I can to persuade Elizabeth to move elsewhere. She needs to get out of Kinnell's reach. I'll write to let you know how I get on."

Chalmers sighed, a soft gust of mingled relief and sadness. "Thank you. Though I doubt I'll see any letter you send me once you're there."

"Of course you will—"

Chalmers waved an admonitory finger at him. "No lies, David, please. Not between us."

David swallowed against the sudden lump in his throat, then forced himself to nod, and Chalmers managed a weak smile in reply.

The silence that followed was broken only by Chalmers's laboured breathing. David watched him, noting the tiny facial clues—the faint furrowing between his brows, the tightness of his mouth—that hinted at the pain he was suffering.

After a while, Chalmers roused himself to speak again. "She talks a lot about this Euan MacLennan. I think they may be living in the same house."

His tone was neutral, impossible to read.

"I believe so."

A brief lull, then, "Do you think she loves him?" Chalmers's gaze was troubled.

"I don't know," David said. Then, driven to honesty: "But I know he loves her. And he is a good man. As far from Kinnell as a man can be."

Chalmers gazed at the ceiling, pondering that.

"When you see her," he said at last, his voice dropped almost to a whisper, "tell her—tell her that I'm sorry I allowed Kinnell to propose to her. I never liked the look of him, and I should have gone with my gut instead of being swayed by Margaret's wishes."

"I'll tell her."

"And tell her I want her to be happy—above all else. If she loves MacLennan, she should have him. It's not her fault that she can't marry him." His eyes drooped again as he rested back against the pillows, breathing shallowly. He was exhausted now, paper white, with a sheen of perspiration on his brow. Yet he steeled himself to speak once more. "Tell her about—about Mary," he said.

"I will," David murmured, covering one frail hand with his own. "I promise."

"You are a good man, David."

"I don't know about that."

"Oh, you are. I can never tell you how grateful I am for what you did for my girl. You needn't have done it. I don't know if I'd've done it, in your shoes. But it's how you are. You see the wrong and the right in the world, and you feel responsible for making it better."

"That's a generous view of me," David said, embarrassed by the older man's breathless, heartfelt words. "Lord Murdo scolds me when I get on my high horse. He says I'm too black-and-white about everything." He chuckled, and Chalmers smiled in return.

"Perhaps at times," he allowed. "Certainly, you're very hard on yourself. I wish you'd let yourself be happy."

That surprised him. He stared at Chalmers, wide-eyed. "I *am* happy," he protested.

"Are you? You're a fine lawyer, lad, but I worry that's all you have in your life. Work."

David felt himself flush. "My work is important to me. It brings me great satisfaction."

"I know. But it is not all there is in life. You realise that?"

Chalmers would never know, David thought, how much more difficult that question was for a man like him. It was easy enough for a man—a normal man—to say *Yes, there is more to life than work* when the *more* he yearns for is marriage to a woman, his own hearth, his own children. But when a man's *more* is something entirely forbidden? When his *more* means embracing a life made up of long, solitary waiting broken up with bright moments of stolen happiness?

David realised Chalmers still waited for his reply, and he made himself smile, though his heart ached. "I do," he said. "I do realise it."

"I hope so," Chalmers whispered. "Because you deserve to be happy, lad. Same as everyone, and more than most."

Chalmers fell into a delirious sort of doze after that, while David considered what the man had said to him, and the words he'd been asked to pass on to Elizabeth.

Be happy. Don't let love go.
Don't deny it.

After twenty minutes, David began to wonder if Chalmers would ever wake. Concerned, he rang the bell, and soon Mrs. Jessop appeared.

"Should I have called before?" David asked anxiously as she bent over Chalmers.

"No, sir," Mrs. Jessop replied, adjusting the pillows. "He is in and out of sleep almost constantly now. Sleep is a blessing for him, you see, a safe harbour from the pain."

David nodded, fighting the ache that grew in his chest as the realisation of his friend's mortality struck him anew.

"I should go now and leave him to his rest."

He stepped forward to touch one last time the thin, dry hand that rested on the bedcovers. The tears in his throat tasted hot and salty.

"Good-bye, old friend," he whispered.

Beneath his fingers, Chalmers's hand stirred, just a tiny movement, then his papery eyelids cracked open.

"Be happy, lad," he breathed. Then closed his eyes once more.

Chapter Seven

Once David was out of Chalmers's house, he set to walking, needing the distraction of physical exercise. He walked east, out past Waterloo Place and up to the broad summit of the Calton Hill, where he sat for a long time, letting the wind rip through his hair, growing so cold he felt almost numb. He probably looked like a statue, sitting on his boulder, unmoving, but inside he was all agitation and grief.

Perhaps if he'd been his old self, he'd have set off running or climbed some rocks. Done something that cost him physically, relishing the burn in his muscles, even a few bruises or cuts. But he wasn't his old self. Even after this relatively short walk, his knee and his hip griped at him.

For once, he was glad of the cane that spared his knee on the descent from the hill. He remembered too vividly each torturous step he'd made on that ill-judged walk back to Laverock House from McNally's, the agonising jolt in his knee each time his right leg had to take his weight. He still felt a shadow of that pain today, but thankfully the cane did the brunt of the work.

It seemed he was learning to be careful after all.

For some reason, that thought depressed him, and when he reached the bottom of the hill, he set off in a new direction, unwilling to return to the house yet. The North Bridge took him up to his old hunting grounds at St. Giles on the High Street. He paused outside Parliament House and debated going in to the advocates' library to see who was around, perhaps to catch up with the latest faculty gossip. In the end, though, he couldn't face it. Couldn't face answering questions about his accident, his recuperation, the reason he was in Edinburgh. Instead, he sloped off to the Tolbooth Tavern and, despite the hour, ordered himself a gill of the hard stuff.

It was gloomy in the tavern. The day was grey and overcast. Even if it had been bright, the tiny windows with their thick, warped glass let in little sun. The only other source of light in the room was the fire in the grate, and that gave off little illumination—it must have been going for a few hours at least, as it was naught but glowing embers now.

Chilled to the bone, David sat himself near the fire. The landlord brought his gill of whisky over, setting down beside it a small metal cup. He acknowledged David's murmured thanks with a nod and tossed a couple of logs onto the fire on his way back to the bar. Soon, yellow tongues of flame were licking over the fresh fuel. Brownish smoke billowed out of the fireplace as the damp, resiny bark was consumed, making David cough and shift his stool back till the logs began burning properly.

He watched as the logs were gradually consumed, first turning black, then glowing orange, then finally going white at the edges, till there was nothing left of them but two ghosts that still somehow held their old shapes—at least until the landlord stirred the fire with a poker and turned them to ash.

It was only then that David blinked himself out of his daze and realised how much time had passed. Realised too that he hadn't so much as poured himself a single dram. His whisky sat, untouched, in the pot jug the landlord had set down in front of him, and the drinking cup was dry.

For a moment he considered sinking the lot in one big gulp. Then he remembered Murdo's hand on his arm, his voice tight with frustration.

"Whenever you're confronted with something you don't like, this is your answer…"

Cursing inwardly, he grabbed his cane and stood, gritting his teeth against the inevitable twinge of pain as he rose. Even with the cane, the long walk had taken its toll on him—in some ways, the hard, uneven cobbles of the city's streets were more punishing than even the worst of country paths.

It wasn't much more than a mile back to Murdo's house, but it felt ten times longer. By the time he crossed the threshold, his limp had returned. The housekeeper came into the hall while the footman was taking his hat and cane. She asked if David would like some luncheon, or perhaps some tea and cake. He smiled politely and declined. Between the emotional encounter with Chalmers and the pain in his hip and knee, he had no appetite at all. He wanted nothing more than to lie down.

At last he was able to excuse himself, escaping to his appointed bedchamber. He near groaned with relief when he finally closed the door behind him, crossing the room to pull the drapes closed. Once his privacy was assured, he stripped his clothes away and sat on the bed to examine his throbbing knee. It was faintly swollen and tender, the pain beginning to worsen now that the constant movement of walking had come to an end and the limb had begun to cool. Sighing, he fetched his jar of liniment from the armoire and began to rub his leg down, reflecting all the while on how much better Murdo was at this, how much more soothing his hands were than David's own.

When he was done, he lay back, grimacing as he arched his stiff hips up so he could drag the top bedcover out from under him and pull it over his exhausted body. Despite his physical tiredness, his mind kept running on, a strange, anxious misery twisting inside him as he considered Chalmers's parting advice to him and his own depressing vision of what his future held.

Months ago, before David's accident, Murdo had alluded to some kind of arrangement whereby they might see each other once a year or so, with Murdo's other life—the one that would have a wife and family in it—kept carefully separate. David didn't need to try that arrangement out to know it wasn't one that he could live with. Everything in him protested at the very thought. When Murdo married, he would make a promise to his wife to cleave only to her. How could David give himself to Murdo after that? It would be wrong in every way. Unfair to Murdo's wife and, yes, unfair to himself too.

He could just imagine Murdo's response to that protest. He'd say that any woman he married would go into the marriage accepting—indeed expecting—that Murdo would have lovers. And that she could take lovers of her own. He would say, in that slightly weary tone he used when talking about the aristocratic world he inhabited, *it's the way of the world...* David had heard it before—It hadn't been enough to allay his objections then, and it wasn't now.

At some point, he fell into an uneasy sleep, drifting into a garbled maze of dreams. He dreamt he was with his first love, Will Lennox, swimming in the river at Midlauder, gooseflesh rising on his skin. Will was young and beautiful, his brown hair sleek from the water, green eyes twinkling with mischief. They came together in a kiss, laughing.

The kiss was innocent at first, but soon it grew more feverish and the body under David's hands grew harder and more demanding. He realised he was no longer with Will but with Murdo.

Murdo's jet gaze met his own, dark and pleading.

David broke the kiss and asked him what was wrong, but Murdo didn't answer him, just gazed at him with mute pain. Then David glanced down and saw that Murdo was bleeding, his long fingers spread over a gaping wound in his chest. David yelled Murdo's name and pressed his own hands over the wound too, crying out helplessly as dark blood slugged out over their interlaced fingers.

He woke himself with his own shouting, his heart thundering with panic and fear, tears wet on his face. At the same moment, his bedchamber door flew open, the handle banging against the wall as Murdo ran in.

"What's wrong?"

David sat up. "Nothing—I just had a dream—a nightmare." He dashed the tears away, mortified. "I'm sorry if I alarmed you."

Murdo's shoulders relaxed, and he closed the door quietly behind himself. "I thought you were being murdered!" he joked as he approached the bed, giving a short, awkward laugh.

Settling himself on the mattress beside David, he added more gently, "Are you all right?"

"In truth, I feel quite shaky," David replied, forcing a laugh. He wanted to ask Murdo to hold him but couldn't find a form of words he could utter. *Will you hold me* was impossible.

It turned out, though, that he didn't need to turn his need into a spoken plea. Murdo reached for him without being asked, his arms sliding round David's slim body, gathering him close.

"Christ, you're freezing," he muttered into David's ear and began chafing David's cold skin with his big, warm hands. "Were you sleeping like that? With just that thin cover over you?"

"I only meant to doze for a few minutes," David said. "But I think I ended up sleeping for quite a while. What time is it?"

"Just gone five."

"I slept three hours, then," David exclaimed, shocked.

"Did you see Chalmers?" Murdo's gaze, dark as pitch and soft with concern, was so reminiscent of the nightmare that David's heart began to race again. Breaking eye contact, he burrowed closer in, needing the physical reassurance of Murdo's body, warm and alive and close to his own. He slid his arms round Murdo's waist and pressed his face into the other man's neck, breathing in his familiar, heady scent.

For a moment, Murdo was very still, as though surprised. Then his arms tightened round David's cold body, and he turned his head to press a kiss against one temple.

And right then, David felt a bolt of unexpected gratitude. Gratitude that he and Murdo were alive. Alive and here, together, now.

A profound understanding settled on him of what it meant to be alive. What a privilege it was. What it meant to share the moments of his life—even the difficult moments—with someone he loved.

Someone I love.

Murdo.

The revelation remained unspoken, the unused words even harder to utter than *Will you hold me?* Easier by far just to stay where he was, holding on to the flesh-and-blood man, imperfectly communicating his feelings by touch.

After a long while, he realised he hadn't answered Murdo's question.

"Sorry, I'm still half-asleep, I think. I did see Chalmers. He made a request of me. I'll need to talk to you about it later."

"We can talk about it now, if you like."

"No, first I—" David paused, struggling again to find words. The ones he picked sounded raw and desperate. "First, I need you."

He lifted his head, knowing his face would give

everything away. He didn't even try to disguise his feelings, though. He just let Murdo see it all, the despair and the grief, and the sharp, pressing desire. Because what was the point in hiding it? What was the point of having the gift of life—and the gift of knowing how precious it was—if he couldn't share it all with this man?

Murdo met David's eyes, and his own gaze gentled. "I need you too," he whispered, and he dipped his head to capture David's lips.

It was just breathing at first; their lips resting together, the air from their mouths mingling. Impossible intimacy. Impossible tenderness. So unbearably sweet it was a barb in David's heart. He felt it like physical pain, like physical joy.

They broke apart briefly, staring at one another, then David leaned in and took Murdo's mouth again, but this time his kiss was hungry, devouring, and after a moment's hesitation, Murdo returned his passion. Their tongues twined, Murdo's clothed body moving against David's naked one, his big hands tracing over David's cold skin.

As good as Murdo's hands felt, David was glad when the other man finally pulled away long enough to shed his clothes. He watched Murdo hungrily as the man quickly stripped, moaning his gratitude when they were finally skin to skin, loving the satiny drag of flesh on flesh and the prickle of Murdo's chest hair against his own mostly smooth torso. He loved the breath-stealing pleasure when their cocks first met, the prod of Murdo's blunt cockhead against the base of his own shaft, the firm press of all that heft as Murdo canted his lean hips up. They ground their shafts together, their mouths meshed in a deep, desperate kiss—breathing the same air, moving to the same frantic rhythm—and it felt like mere moments till David was crying out his release, Murdo's answering groan following a heartbeat behind.

Afterwards, they lay in companionable silence for a long time. At last, though, Murdo turned his head on the pillow.

"So, what did Chalmers want?"

David repeated what Chalmers had told him about Kinnell's visit to Charles Carr, and his request that David deal with moving the trust administration.

"I have to get to London as soon as possible," he said when he was finished. "I want you to take me with you tomorrow." He noted Murdo's faint frown and added, "I cannot rest easy until I've fulfilled my promise, Murdo."

"David Lauriston to the rescue once again," Murdo observed, his tone very dry. "You'll be wanting me to saddle my best white horse for you, will you?"

"I'm merely undertaking the duties of my office as trustee—" David began, breaking off when Murdo sighed.

"All right, all right," the other man said. "I know better than to try to dissuade you once you've made your mind up. You'll have to pack your things this evening though. We leave at first light."

Chapter Eight

Another carriage journey. This one, though, was farther than David had ever travelled before. Until now, he'd had no cause to go anywhere that involved more than two days by carriage. London was taking the better part of a week, and it felt like the longest week of David's life.

Murdo had assured David that if the inns Murdo had reserved had no spare bedchambers, no one would blink an eye at the two of them bunking together. David had almost looked forward to the prospect, only for it to turn out that, by some twist of fortune, the inns *all* had spare bedchambers. Not to mention nosy landlords and fellow guests who traipsed the corridors at all hours of the night. Consequently, David and Murdo had spent the last five days in torturous proximity—together all day in the swaying, closed-in carriage, knowing they could be interrupted at any moment, only to be separated each night.

They'd passed the time talking. At long last, Murdo began to break some of the careful conversational rules he'd set months before, when David had first gone to Laverock House. Not that David could really call them rules. Murdo had never explicitly said there were things he would not discuss. He was just good at making it plain when he wasn't happy talking about a particular subject. And he was never happy talking about his family.

Until now, it seemed. On this journey, he finally began to speak about them—about his siblings, anyway. About his older brothers, dutiful Harris and pompous Iain, neither of whom Murdo much liked, and about his three younger sisters, all of whom were married to men handpicked by Murdo's father. He learned about Murdo's late mother too, a kindly but distant figure from Murdo's childhood who'd had no time for her youngest son as she coped with pregnancy after pregnancy, a succession of new babies and stillbirths, until she finally succumbed to the rigours of childbirth when Murdo was thirteen.

He barely mentioned his father, though, beyond alluding to him as the strategist of each of his children's dynastic marriages or as the architect of his sons-in-law's political careers. Murdo didn't need to say much, though, for David to understand that the Marquess of Balfour cast a long shadow over his son's life. Nor to realise that the marquess had something to do with this journey. He'd worked that out weeks ago.

The marquess was a prolific letter writer. Each

week, at least one, sometimes two letters arrived at Laverock House. David had quickly come to recognise the heavy, off-white paper, the lavish seal and the precise pen work that marked the earl's correspondence. Whenever David arrived at the breakfast table and saw one of those distinctive letters waiting, he knew that Murdo would take it away to read it privately. And that soon after, the subject of Murdo going to London would crop up.

"Susannah's far too young for Lansbury," Murdo was saying now. Susannah was his youngest and favourite sister. "She never got the chance to go to balls and have admirers, and, of course, now she wants to do it as a young matron, except Lansbury won't have it."

"Why did your father select a man so *much* older than her?" David asked. "Surely there must've been at least one man closer to her in age who would've been suitable?"

Murdo snorted. "It wouldn't even have crossed his mind to wonder. He wanted to align himself to Lansbury, and Lansbury wanted a wife. Why not his eighteen-year-old daughter, even if Lansbury was thirty years older?"

"I'm surprised he's not managed to marry you off yet, if he's so ruthless," David said. He'd begun mentioning the marquess more directly over the last day or two, curious to see if he could coax Murdo into saying more about his father.

As was usual when David mentioned the earl, Murdo's jaw tightened and he looked away, out of the window of the carriage. But just when David thought that was it, that the conversation was at an end, Murdo said, "It's not for want of effort."

"What do you mean?"

Murdo kept his gaze trained on the flat, dull landscape outside. "My father's like a spider," he said eventually. "His web goes on and on. I've been snipping at the threads all my life." After a pause, he turned his head to look at David again and smiled, though it was no more than a tightening of his lips. No warmth reached his eyes. "Let's not talk of him. It makes me peevish."

It made him more than peevish, David thought. It made him unhappy.

To distract him, David began to ask questions about their surroundings and soon enough Murdo was telling him all about the county of Buckinghamshire, reciting the names of the local families who owned the greatest tracts of land in the area. He did it almost by rote, as though he'd learned it a long time ago. David listened, occasionally asking a further question, more interested in Murdo's immediate yet oddly disinterested way of answering than in the answers themselves.

He'd been tutored in this.

After a little while, the carriage began to slow. David stuck his head out of the window, ascertaining they were approaching their next stop, an old, rambling coaching inn. Its roof looked recently thatched, and it had a sturdy, prosperous look about it. It was by far the nicest inn they'd stayed in since they'd left Edinburgh. Curling wisps of wood smoke trailed from the chimneys and hung in the darkening sky, not seeming to know where to go.

As though alerted to the proximity of food, David's stomach let out a tremendous rumble, making Murdo chuckle.

"Hungry?" he asked.

"I've had nothing since breakfast," David pointed out, his tone faintly defensive. He'd refused food at their previous stops, nauseated by the long hours in the swaying carriage. The afternoon leg of the journey had been easier on his stomach, though, and now his belly was complaining at its emptiness. Loudly.

The coachman expertly swung the team of four and the broad carriage through the inn's narrow gate without so much as grazing a corner. And then it was the same routine they'd followed for the last few nights. They got out of the carriage while their trunks were unloaded by the inn's servants and the ostlers unhitched the horses, and headed for the main body of the inn in search of the innkeeper.

They found him in the hallway, on his way out to meet them, a small, wiry man of indeterminate age, his thick, nut-brown hair belied by a deeply wrinkled face.

David wondered if he wore a wig.

He had an obsequious manner that grated on David. It was probably necessary in his line of work, given the number of well-to-do customers he'd have who'd expect to be treated with proper respect, but there was something about his manner that verged on grovelling.

He introduced himself as Mr. Foster, and his eyes lit up when Murdo confirmed his own identify.

"Ah, Your *Lordship*," he said, with relish. "We've been expecting you."

"You've been expecting myself and my coachman," Murdo corrected. "But not Mr. Lauriston here. Are you able to assist us with an additional bedchamber?"

Foster smiled, displaying a set of strong-looking, yellow teeth, and, disappointingly, confirmed a second bedchamber presented no difficulty all. Murdo—ever accustomed to giving orders and expecting them to be carried out—demanded that hot baths be prepared for both of them and dinner served in a private parlour. Foster smoothly agreed to all of Murdo's commands.

Within twenty minutes of their arrival, David was stripping off his travel-rumpled clothes and lowering himself into a blessedly hot bath, his first in days. The heat eased his pinched knee—always made worse by inactivity—making him sigh with pleasure and relief.

He stayed in the water till it was practically cold. When he finally got out, he quickly dried himself off, then gave his leg a brisk rub with liniment before dressing again. When he ventured out of his room, he felt cleaner and more relaxed than he had in days. He made his way to the private parlour Murdo had reserved, sniffing appreciatively as he went—the scents emerging from the kitchens were very promising—to find the innkeeper himself waiting outside the parlour door.

When Foster saw David, he greeted him with the same servility that had made David shudder earlier, even tugging at his forelock before opening the door for him. David gave him a curt nod and passed him.

The parlour was a cosy room, twee even. Murdo looked quite out of place in it, surrounded by floral china and Toby jugs and framed needlepoint pictures. He was too big, too male. A wolf in a woodcutter's cottage. David smiled at his own whimsy and walked farther into the room, noticing with pleasure that Murdo's expression warmed when he saw David. He suspected his own did the same.

The door closed behind them and immediately Murdo's expression became less guarded. He quickly stepped up to David and captured his mouth in a quick but thorough kiss, his big hand resting at David's waist. When he pulled back, his eyes were dancing.

"We shouldn't," David said, as though Murdo had posed a question. Despite his reluctant words, though, he was grinning, almost dizzy with happiness at Murdo's brief, seemingly helpless show of affection.

They'd shared little more than a few such kisses since they'd left Edinburgh, and this was the first night they'd managed to secure a private parlour for dinner. The closed door and drawn curtains made their privacy feel more secure than it possibly was.

"Probably not," Murdo agreed merrily, adding, "Did you enjoy your bath? You look as though you did. You're all pink-cheeked and shiny."

"The bath was wonderful," David assured him gravely. "I stayed in so long my fingers were like prunes when I got out."

"Me too." Murdo grinned. "And I have high hopes for dinner. The food doesn't smell half-bad."

As though he'd heard them—and perhaps he had—Foster chose that moment to enter, bearing a basket of new-baked bread in one hand and a dish of butter in the other.

"Good evening, my lord," he said with a deep bow to Murdo. He looked odd, bowing like that with the basket and butter dish still in his hands. He turned to offer a smaller bow to David. "Sir."

David nodded and murmured a "good evening" of his own, but it was lost as Murdo bit out angrily, "I thought you said this was a *private* parlour?"

The innkeeper blanched, freezing in the midst of straightening from his bow. "I beg your pardon, my lord?"

"You damn well ought to!" Murdo continued. "Haven't you heard of knocking before you enter a private room?"

David swallowed, suddenly mortified. Could Murdo make it any more obvious that they craved privacy? Then he dismissed his own thoughts impatiently. Murdo was right. It *was* meant to be a private parlour, and Foster wouldn't necessarily assume that, just because his male guests wanted privacy, they wanted one another. They could simply be discussing private business.

"Well?" Murdo snapped.

"Please accept my apologies, my lord," Foster stammered. "I forgot myself for a moment. It won't happen again."

It didn't. Foster stayed away after that, and the nervous young serving maid he sent in his place nearly knocked the door down each time she brought a new dish, her hands shaking as she laid the rattling crockery down. Murdo was polite to her, though. Gentle even.

There was a bit of a disaster when she brought the gravy. She was balancing too many things, and the sauce boat overturned, upsetting its contents all over the white tablecloth.

"Oh no!" she gasped. "Mr. Foster'll have me guts for garters!"

Flushing scarlet, she began trying to wipe up the mess with her apron.

Murdo put a hand on her arm to still her. "What's

your name, girl?"

"Peggy, m'lor'," she said, looking at him obediently, though her anxious gaze flitted back to the table.

"Right then, Peggy," Murdo said firmly. "Go back to the kitchen and tell Mr. Foster that His Lordship overturned the gravy boat, and now he wants a fresh tablecloth brought and this one burned. And the cost is to be added to my bill, if you please." He said it all in his most supercilious tone, giving the girl the right words to parrot to her master, then he smiled his most coaxing smile. "Do you have that?"

She stared at him, eyes wide, and repeated what he said. Twice through, at Murdo's insistence. When he was satisfied, he released her, and she scurried away.

Once she was gone, Murdo turned to David. "What?" he said. "Why are you looking at me like that?"

"That was kind," David said simply, then he chuckled. "And not a little devious."

"Devious?" Murdo's tone was outraged, but his expression was amused, the winsome dimple that David loved making a rare appearance.

"I wouldn't have approached it like that. I'd have spoken to Foster on her behalf instead." David paused, then admitted, "I'd probably have made it worse for her."

Murdo chuckled. "Honest to a fault, that's you."

David chuckled too, ruefully. "That's what my

mother's always said about me."

"You're direct," Murdo said. "Uncompromising."

"You think me inflexible," David accused without heat.

Murdo inclined his head. "At times. Sometimes I hesitate to tell you things because—" He stopped, his gaze suddenly troubled.

"Because what?"

"You're very black-and-white about everything. I've never met anyone who has such a strong sense of right and wrong."

David considered that echo of Chalmers's words from a few days before. "I'm not sure that's true," he said, frowning. "I struggle more than anyone I know with what's right and wrong."

"That's just it, though," Murdo said. "Most people don't worry about it all that much. Most people are adept at convincing themselves that what they want—what suits them—is right. Or at least, that it isn't really wrong." He smiled. "*I'm* adept at that."

David sipped his ale. "I really don't think I'm as principled as you imagine," he said at last. "Over the last year or two, my views on certain things have altered significantly—in ways that have suited me very well."

Murdo's gaze gentled. "If you're talking about us, I know you didn't alter your view without a struggle. In fact, I know you still struggle with it, still question yourself." He paused, then added, "I know that, even now, when you give yourself to me, you hold a part of yourself back."

David's heart clenched at that, and at that bleak look in the other man's eyes. What Murdo said was true, but he hadn't realised Murdo knew it.

"I feel as though—" Murdo began, then stopped, seeming to debate with himself whether to continue. When he started up again, his tone was careful. "I feel as though we're fighting over that part of you. I want you to give it up, give it to me. But you're still not convinced that what we have together is—right. And I don't know what I can do to convince you."

"Murdo—"

The knock at the door was different this time, harder, with a flourishing rhythm at the end, *tat-tat-te-tat-tat*.

They glanced at one another, both frustrated by the interruption. "Come in," Murdo called out.

It was Foster this time, with Peggy trailing behind him, a clean tablecloth over her arm and a miserable expression on her plump face.

"Your Lordship requested a clean tablecloth?" Foster said with unctuous smile.

Murdo gave the little man a long look, before he confirmed. "I did," he said. "And that you proceed to burn this one, if you please." He flicked a disdainful finger at the stained one.

"Of course," Foster assured him, and began to remove the silverware from the table before adding casually, "I must apologise for Peggy's clumsiness."

He had guessed it was the girl, David realised, and had come to prod out the truth.

He had made a grave error.

"I *beg* your pardon?" Murdo's incredulous voice was pure ice.

Foster stilled in what he was doing and looked up. Seeing the expression on Murdo's face, he swallowed hard.

"What *exactly* do you mean by that comment?" Murdo demanded.

"I was merely apologising, my lord," Foster said, licking his lips nervously. "I've no doubt the girl caused you to spill the gravy, and I wanted to assure you—"

"What did she tell you?" Murdo demanded.

It was plain that Foster took Murdo's swift question as evidence that his suspicions were warranted—his eyes gleamed with triumph. "Merely that, my lord. That you spilled the gravy and wanted a new tablecloth."

"And to add the cost of the ruined one to my bill?"

"Yes."

"Then why are you bothering me?" Murdo roared at him, eyes flashing and nostrils flaring with temper.

Foster quaked in the face of Murdo's impressive anger, while Peggy, who stood behind the innkeeper, looked at the floor, biting her lip against a tiny smile.

"Perhaps," Murdo went on, "you think to chide *me* for my clumsiness? Is that it? Are these apologies a backhanded way of giving me a scold?"

"No! No, my lord! I would not presume to criticise!" the innkeeper babbled.

"I've already said I'll pay for a new tablecloth. Is that not enough for you?"

"My lord, it is most *generous*," Foster went on, his expression growing more horrified by the second. "I did not intend to suggest that your spilling gravy was in any way careless."

Murdo waved him away impatiently. "Enough of this. Pray, leave us." He gestured to Peggy. "And you, girl, attend to the table, if you please." Then, entirely ignoring Foster, he turned to David and began to talk about, of all things, horses.

Foster slunk away, while Peggy began to clear the remaining dishes to the sideboard. Once the door had closed behind Foster and a minute or two had passed, Murdo turned to the girl again.

"He didn't believe you, I take it?"

She shook her head miserably. "I'm always in trouble with 'im. Always getting me wages docked."

"You should find yourself a new position."

"I'm saving to get married. Just another year and I'll be away."

"Is that so?"

Murdo dug into his pocket and brought out a leather purse, beckoning the girl over. Peggy approached apprehensively.

"Put out your hand," he said.

She opened her hand, and he counted five guineas out into her plump palm.

The girl stared at the gold in her hand, and her other hand crept up to cover her mouth. Tears welled in her eyes. "Oh, sir," she whispered. Then she looked up, horrified. "I mean, my lord!"

"Put it safely away, somewhere that odious little man won't find it. We don't want him to accuse you of stealing, do we? And here—" He drew out one of his cards and handed it to her. "That has my name and direction on it, just in case you have any more difficulties with him before you leave."

"Thank you," she whispered, still staring, awestruck, at the coins.

"You'd better get this lot cleared up before he comes back looking for you." Murdo smiled.

She did as he bid her, wisely slipping the coins into the toe of her shoe first.

Once she was gone, David said, "That was quite a little scene you acted out with Foster. I don't think I've ever seen you being quite so *aristocratic* before."

"Like that, did you?"

"I wouldn't say I *liked* it—I wouldn't like you to act that way with me, at any rate—but it was very effective, I must say."

"It's effective with some people," Murdo admitted. "Rest assured, I wouldn't even bother trying it with an egalitarian like you." He grinned at that, his black eyes gleaming with humour, and David was swamped, quite suddenly, by a wave of helpless love and affection. Love for this complex, sometimes difficult man who was, nevertheless, capable of great kindness.

This man who'd once said to David, *"Don't try to find a virtue in me, Lauriston. You won't."*

David reached across the white tablecloth and took hold of Murdo's hand, lifting it up to his mouth to graze a kiss across the knuckles, loving the warmth of the skin his lips brushed, and the strength in the long fingers that curved about his own.

Murdo looked briefly puzzled by David's affectionate behaviour, but when David went to draw away, he tightened his hold on David's hand, and they stayed like that for a long while, finishing their ale and watching the fire burn down to nothing but ash.

Chapter Nine

The clattering of horses and carriages in the inn's courtyard began before the clock struck five the next morning. Groaning, David pulled a pillow over his face to shut out the noise, but it was no good. Soon enough, there were maidservants going up and down stairs and guests moving around, and David gave up all hope of any further rest.

He wished he at least had Murdo with him. They could have spent an hour or two together in bed. As it was, David found himself indulging in something he'd had no need to resort to for some time, bringing himself to a perfunctory climax with his own hand.

He got up straight after, washing and dressing without so much as looking in the mirror, tucking his overlong hair behind his ears and tying his cravat in its usual slapdash knot.

Murdo was in the breakfast parlour when he got downstairs, looking as tired and grumpy as David felt, albeit ten times as elegant. He grunted at David over his plate of kippers and suggested they make an earlier start than planned, given they were up, a suggestion David was only too happy to agree to.

The final leg of their journey was actually quite pleasant. They were only a few hours from London, and after a hearty breakfast and near enough a pot of coffee each, they were well fed and alert—for the time being, anyway, till tiredness caught up with them. By shortly after noon, Murdo's carriage was pulling up outside Murdo's London townhouse on Curzon Street.

David climbed out of the carriage, using his cane to avoid putting too much strain on his bad leg, ignoring Murdo's approving smile. Once he stood on the pavement, he gazed around, fascinated. The townhouses that lined the street were remarkably similar to those at home, with the same classical facades, but here they varied in height, some of them a full storey or more higher than their neighbours.

The colour palette of these buildings varied too, brown brick and bright-white stucco. Very different from the ubiquitous sandstone which gave Edinburgh its characteristically gloomy beauty. It struck David, as he looked about him, that the sober townhouses of his home city were more elegant than this—collectively, at least. The unified lines of Edinburgh's New Town, the sweeping crescents and classical perfection, were incomparable. Yet these houses, too high, too grand, spoke of something different, something entirely less collective. No New Town here. Here, they built what they wanted, where they wanted it, setting down their lofty houses in the middle of the city, right on top of whatever had been there before. A statement of individual pride and wealth.

"Come on," Murdo said, touching David's elbow. Realising he'd become absorbed in his own thoughts, David gave a self-conscious laugh and followed Murdo up the steps to the house.

The door was opened by a thin little man with bright, watchful eyes, sallow skin and neatly combed iron-grey hair—Liddle, Murdo called him. The man bowed to Murdo, welcoming him home in a quiet, precise voice.

"This is Mr. Lauriston," Murdo advised his butler. "My new secretary."

Liddle bowed to David, his expression devoid of curiosity. David fought the urge to bow back, settling for inclining his head more respectfully than was probably strictly proper.

The butler turned back to Murdo. "Shall I prepare the Blue Room for Mr. Lauriston, my lord?"

"No," Murdo said. "The Green."

David's gaze flickered between the two men. Liddle merely nodded at Murdo's instruction, and already David could see that the man was far too discreet to react in any way to anything he heard. But David wondered if he'd detected a ripple of interest. Something, perhaps about the way the man studiously *didn't* look at David in response to Murdo's order. A brief glance might have been expected had Murdo merely agreed with the servant's suggestion, mightn't it? Or perhaps David was being oversensitive? Perhaps Liddle truly thought nothing of it?

"We'll take some refreshments in the drawing room just now," Murdo informed the butler, resting his hand at the small of David's back and urging him forward. David felt that hand like a brand, a prickle of discomfort going up his spine as he wondered what the butler made of them.

Already David could see that this house was quite unlike the one in Edinburgh. The Edinburgh house was plush and masculine, with solid, comfortable furniture. This was far more elegant and far more formal, everything sharp and bright and hard-edged. The drawing room that Murdo led David into was twice the size of an ordinary room. The fireplace was huge, carved from white marble, and the walls were pale blue up to the picture rail, the expensive wallpaper reflecting the light like frost. Above the picture rail, everything was white. David looked up, his eyes drawn first to the ornate cornicing, and then to the crystal chandelier that hung from the plaster ceiling rose, its droplets sparkling like ice. It was a beautiful room, but cold. Even the furniture was cold, upholstered in spotless, ivory satin, making David conscious of his crumpled, dusty travel clothes.

"Stop fretting and sit down," Murdo said, sounding amused. He had already settled himself into the largest armchair in the room, by the fireplace. After a moment, David crossed to the sofa opposite Murdo, dusting off the tails of his coat before carefully lowering himself down.

"How's your leg?"

"Not too bad," David replied. In truth, his leg ached but talking about his injury was beginning to bore him.

"Perhaps it's done you a bit of good to rest it," Murdo said. "You may have been overdoing the exercise."

"I feel better when I exercise it though," David replied. "I'll be glad to get back to walking again." He yawned broadly, and a moment later, Murdo did too, making them both grin. "My sleepiness is catching," David observed.

"Perhaps we should have an afternoon nap?" Murdo suggested, cocking a suggestive brow, the corner of his generous mouth twitching appealingly.

David sighed with genuine regret. "I should really go over to Blackfriars as soon as I can," he said, adding after a pause, "I'll walk over there this afternoon."

Murdo's grin faded at that, but he didn't protest. "At least take the carriage," he said. "It's miles away, and you don't know London at all."

"It's only a couple of miles. It'll take me an hour at

most, and in truth I'd like to see a bit of the city on foot. I promise to take my cane."

"I'll come with you, then."

"I don't think that's a good idea," David murmured. Euan was living in the same house as Elizabeth, and even though Murdo had indirectly helped Elizabeth escape from Kinnell, the last occasion on which the two men had seen one another was two years before, when Euan had been holding a gun to David's head. Despite everything that had happened since then, David suspected that Murdo still didn't trust Euan and that he wouldn't trouble to hide his feelings. David would have enough to deal with, giving Elizabeth the news about her father, without having to worry about anything else.

Murdo pressed his lips together. David could tell he was desperate to say something—probably to try to lay down the law—but was somehow managing to stop himself. Over the months they'd spent together at Laverock House, Murdo had come to realise that he couldn't make David do what he wanted with either verbal demands or coercion, and seeing his lover's reluctant acceptance of that was amusing and oddly touching.

David stayed deliberately quiet for a while, allowing Murdo to simmer in peace, while his own mind drifted ahead to what he would say to Elizabeth and Euan about Chalmers. How did one break news like that? He considered and discarded a dozen different openings.

Eventually, a footman entered the dining room bearing a heavily loaded tray, which Murdo ordered him to place on the table before dismissing the man.

"If you're going to insist on going over to Blackfriars before dinner, at least eat something first," Murdo said, putting a buttered crumpet and a slice of seed cake on a delicate china plate and handing it to David.

David grinned as he accepted the plate, amused by the oddly domestic gesture.

"And you can stop laughing," Murdo added through gritted teeth.

To reward him for his restraint, David ate two more crumpets and a second slice of cake, silently noting Murdo's quiet satisfaction with puzzled amusement.

When he was done, he leaned back in his chair and yawned so widely he felt his jaw might crack. When he straightened again, Murdo was smiling at him, an odd expression in his dark eyes.

"You're tired," Murdo observed.

"I doubt I slept more than four hours last night," David admitted. "But I'll catch up tonight."

Murdo watched him for a moment. "I know you're keen to get going, but you'd benefit from a short nap first. Why don't you go up to your bedchamber? I won't join you, and I'll make sure you're woken in an hour."

David opened his mouth to protest, only to yawn hugely again. "That might be an idea," he admitted, and Murdo reached for the bellpull.

Within a minute or two, Liddle was back. He carried a silver tray bearing a thick bundle of correspondence for Murdo.

"You called, my lord?" he said quietly as he placed the tray on a small table at Murdo's right hand.

"Yes, would you show Mr. Lauriston to his chamber?"

"Of course, my lord." The butler turned to David. "Would you follow me, sir?"

David rose stiffly from his chair, his knee protesting a bit as he reached for his cane.

"And make sure you rub that leg down," Murdo said firmly, making David's cheeks heat as he wondered what Liddle thought of that comment.

Liddle led David upstairs—just one flight, thankfully—and down a short corridor.

"Your bedchamber, sir," the servant said in his quiet, precise voice, standing aside to allow David to precede him, adding, "His Lordship's is next door."

David's cheeks warmed at that comment, but he said nothing, merely walked into the middle of the room, where his open trunk stood.

"Your clothes have been pressed and put away, sir. I trust that meets with your approval?"

David turned, smiling politely. "Yes, thank you." The first time that had happened, David had found it mortifying—the thought of a servant putting away his drawers and shaving things for him—but he'd grown used to it now. It was how things were done.

The butler inclined his head and withdrew, closing the door behind him.

David's first thought was to wonder why it was called the Green Room. The walls were hung with yellow silk wallpaper, and the satin bedcover was yellow too. There was no green anywhere that he could see.

The room felt stuffy to him. He went to the window to lift the sash, and the busy sounds of the city poured in—the rumble of carriages, the clatter of horses' hooves. He pulled the drapes closed over the open window, and they stirred in the breeze, doing nothing to muffle the noise from the street below.

Stripping down to his drawers, David folded back the rich satin bedcover, exposing the sheets and blankets below, and crawled inside. Although he found it difficult to sleep during the day, he was exhausted, and he closed his eyes with every expectation of drifting off. But sleep wouldn't come. He lay there, listening to the clock ticking, his traitorous body refusing to succumb as ten, then twenty, then thirty minutes passed. Eventually, he swore and sat up, swinging his legs out of the bed, reasoning that he may as well go straight to see Elizabeth.

After crossing the room to the armoire, he poured water into the porcelain basin and briskly washed himself before fetching fresh clothes from the wardrobe, grateful that the creases had already been pressed out of them. Once dressed, he studied his face in the mirror, rubbing a hand over his cheeks. He'd shaved that morning at the inn, and although there was a faint roughness of new growth that dragged at his fingertips, he'd get away without shaving again. His too-long hair was tumbling into his eyes, though, and he reached for his jar of pomade to tame it, finger-combing a generous dab of the waxy, resin-scented stuff through his thick, dark-red locks.

When he looked at his reflection in the glass, he was briefly shocked. He'd donned his best black suit of clothes and—for once—exercised some care in the tying of his neckcloth. Between that and his ruthlessly tamed hair, he looked like...well, like the old David Lauriston. A quiet, measured professional man. A bookish sort. Dry and studious, not a bit of passion in him. Not at all like a man who donned his lover's worn-out breeches to go fishing and let his hair grow so long that it hung in his eyes. Not like a man who loved someone of his own sex. No one would think such a thing of the respectable gentleman in the looking glass.

He was still considering his reflection, a frown

marring his brow, when a great rapping came from the street below. David went to the window and twitched the curtain aside to peer down. There was a gentleman standing at the top of the steps, a gold-topped cane—presumably the instrument of that loud knocking—in his hand.

David couldn't make out much of the man from his vantage point, only the top of his black hat and a general impression of elegance and wealth. A moment later, the front door swung open, and the man was admitted.

David waited a few minutes before he went downstairs, enough time for the visitor to be shown into Murdo's presence so that David could slip away without having to be introduced. Once he was satisfied he'd allowed enough time to pass, he put on his hat, picked up his cane and left his bedchamber.

His strategy didn't quite work out. When he reached the bottom of the stairs and crossed the hallway, he discovered that the drawing room door was wide open and that Murdo and his visitor stood just inside the threshold, facing each other. Murdo, the taller of the two, had his arms crossed over his broad chest, a belligerent expression on his face, while his visitor spoke in a low, driven tone, his words indistinct. At the sound of David's cane tapping on the floor, they both turned their heads, and for the briefest instant, before he shielded his expression, Murdo looked horror-stricken.

Shaken by that, David turned his attention to the visitor, quickly realising that if the man wasn't Murdo's father, he had to be another close relative. He was tall and broad, like Murdo, with the same thick hair—once dark, now streaked with grey—and black, flashing eyes. They shared the same shape of head, the same determined chin, but there were differences too. Murdo must have gotten his quick smile and the appealing glint of humour in his ink-black gaze from his mother, because this man had no humour about him at all. Everything about him had a downward cast—the outer corners of his eyes, his long nose, the thin slash of his mouth. It was a forbidding face and, right now, a sneering one.

"Is this him, Murdoch?" the man asked, his gaze raking David from head to toe. "Your latest catamite? The one you've been so reluctant to part yourself from?" His voice dripped with contempt.

The sudden, unexpected insult shocked David like a physical blow, and his gaze snapped to Murdo, who looked so furious David was sure he was about to lose his formidable temper. To David's surprise, though, he pressed his lips together, keeping himself in check, even as a faint flush across his cheekbones and the flaring of nostrils betrayed his agitation.

"I know you have no manners, Father," Murdo said, "but Mr. Lauriston—my *secretary*—is a guest in this house, and I will thank you to show him the respect he deserves."

"Your secretary," the marquess repeated, his tone frankly disbelieving. Then he shook his head and brushed past Murdo, walking farther into the room and sitting himself down on the same chair Murdo had selected earlier. It was the chair, David realised, of the master of the house, occupying as it did the dominant position in the room.

Murdo turned to David. "Go and see your friend," he said quietly. "Liddle will arrange the carriage for you."

"There's no need for Mr. Lauriston to leave," the marquess said behind him in a carrying, cut-glass voice. "I'm not here to discuss matters of state, Murdoch. Nothing I have to say to you needs to be said in private. In fact—"

Murdo turned on him. "Father—" he began, but the marquess went on, heedless of the interruption.

"—it rather seems to me that it's only fair if he stays to hear what I have to say." He gave Murdo a small, cruel smile before turning his gaze on David again. "Don't you agree, Mr. Lauriston?"

David frowned and glanced at Murdo, who was still staring at his father, his expression betraying nothing, though David could detect his suppressed anxiety.

David stayed silent, not responding to the earl. But

neither did he move away. He knew something was coming, something that Murdo didn't want him to hear and that the marquess definitely did, and for the life of him he couldn't walk away, despite knowing this was going to be painful.

"You see," the marquess continued in a deceptively reasonable tone of voice, addressing himself to David this time, "I've been trying to prevail upon Murdoch to come back to London for, oh, about six months now. To fulfil an obligation he undertook almost a year ago."

Murdo glanced at David. "I was going to tell you," he muttered. "I just needed to—" He broke off, and his gaze was bleak.

"Tell me what?" David asked weakly.

"About his engagement," the marquess said. "Murdoch has been engaged to Lady Louisa Hartley since last March. And it's past time the wedding took place."

Chapter Ten

Murdo was engaged to be married—and he'd never said a word about it to David.

All those letters from London...

David perched on the edge of one of the uncomfortable drawing room chairs and stared at his own hands. Out in the hall, the marquess was complaining at being escorted out of the house. No sooner had the marquess made his announcement—and David had murmured some vague words of congratulation—than Murdo had invented another pressing appointment he had to attend. The marquess didn't believe a word of it, but Murdo had somehow herded him out of the room while David hung on to his dignity by a thread, a strained smile on his face.

Another rumble of voices. Murdo's was low and certain, the earl's sharp and querulous. Then the front door closed, and the only sound was Murdo's careful footsteps crossing the hall.

When David looked up, Murdo was standing in the doorway, an expression on his face that David found difficult to read—his mouth was tight and grim, as though he was angry, but his dark eyes were soft with regret. He stepped into the room and closed the door carefully behind him.

For a long moment, they were both silent, then Murdo said, "I'm sorry I didn't tell you."

"Why didn't you?"

"I wanted to fix it before I told you."

"Fix it?"

"Break it off."

David gave a sharp, humourless laugh. "How can you break it off? You're *engaged*. You've made a promise to this Lady Louisa."

Murdo sighed and passed a weary hand over his face. "This is exactly why I didn't tell you," he said. "I knew you'd say that."

David stood up so quickly, his knee felt like a knife had been stuck in it, and he had to grab the back of the chair to steady himself.

"How dare you!" he said. "How *fucking* dare you! You didn't tell me you were engaged—and you knew very well how I'd feel about that."

Murdo looked away, his expression part ashamed, part mutinous. "You think these things are written in stone, David, but the reality is, engagements are quietly terminated all the time."

"The *reality* is, it's a legally binding arrangement, and she's entitled to hold you to it."

"For God's sake, *Lady Louisa Hartley* will not cause a scandal by suing me for breach of promise! That would benefit no one—least of all her. She'd be a laughingstock!" Murdo stepped forward, closing the gap between them. "David, please—I just need a little time to negotiate my way out of this. I'll meet with her father, agree on an appropriate form of compensation, and let him make whatever announcement he wants to ensure Louisa saves face—"

"You think it will be that easy?" David retorted hotly. "With your own father determined that the marriage should proceed?"

Murdo's jaw tightened. "Forget my father. I can deal with him."

David's anger drained away, to be replaced with anxiety. "You're talking about a man who threatened to have you committed to an asylum when you spoke of defying him once before. He knows what you are, and he's shown you he's prepared to use that knowledge against you."

"So I shouldn't try to extricate myself, is that what you're saying? You think I should marry her?" Murdo's expression was grim.

"Christ, I don't know!" David exclaimed. He turned away, running a hand over the back of his neck. "I only learned about this ten minutes ago. What do you want me to say?"

"Honestly?" Murdo snapped. "I rather hoped you

might actually want me to give her up."

David slowly turned back to look at Murdo, staring at him in bewildered astonishment.

"Oh, it's not as though I *expected* you to say that," Murdo added in a bitter tone. "I expected exactly this—for you to tell me I can't get out of the engagement, that I'm honour-bound to go through with the wedding. To keep a fast hold of that precious pride of yours, that part of you that you guard so fucking close."

David's temper returned at that. "You chose to keep this from me," he exclaimed, "and now you expect me to shrug it off within ten minutes?"

"No, of course I don't! I wanted to tell you. But every time I thought about it—hell, I knew it would be like this. I thought if I could just resolve it first, *then* tell you…" He broke off, shaking his head, his eyes on the floor as though he couldn't bear to look at David.

David didn't know what to say. He was angry and grief-stricken. The fact that Murdo had deliberately kept this from him—through all those days and nights together at Laverock House—made him feel sick to his stomach. He wanted to walk out of this house and out of London and keep walking till he reached home.

"I'm going to see Elizabeth," he said, suddenly decisive. "It's probably better if we're apart for a bit." He made for the door, his arm brushing against Murdo's as he passed.

"David—" Murdo said. His voice sounded rusty

and broken, but he didn't put a hand out to detain David, and David didn't look back.

He'd come away without directions to Blackfriars, but he didn't want to return to the house, so he just walked till he came upon a groom tending a gentleman's horse outside another lofty townhouse. Once he'd got used to the man's strong cockney accent, he discovered the way to Blackfriars was simple enough—walk east and stay close to the river, keeping an eye out for the tall steeple of St. Bride's Church to the north.

Even with such simple directions, David felt somewhat disorientated. It was the sheer size of London. Like twenty cities in one, and everything scaled up accordingly. Streets that were miles long and mazes of squares and crescents and lanes. Every now and again, he made sure to stop a passerby to check that he was still going the right way.

It was easier once he had St. Bride's Church's steeple in his sights. The groom had told him that once he'd passed it, Blackfriars was very close, and, sure enough, a talkative costermonger was able to direct him to Shoemaker Row with a few simple instructions. David gave him a penny for a sorry-looking apple in thanks, passing the fruit to a beggar woman he passed a few minutes later.

As he walked on, the streets became shorter and narrower, a labyrinth of lanes whose tall, stooped buildings crowded together like a parliament of crooked old men sharing a fire. There were no cobbles here, just hard-packed dirt lanes riddled with potholes and muddy puddles. The walking was hard on David's leg, and he found himself relying on his cane more than he liked to. He'd left Murdo's house over an hour ago, and the temper that had sent him striding out the door had worn off some way back. Now, he was tired and aching and longing to reach his destination, even as he dreaded carrying out the task that had been given to him.

Elizabeth and Euan lived on a tiny street just off Shoemaker Row. It was a little shabby, but clean and well tended. A group of laughing children played with a couple of spinning tops in the street while their mothers exchanged gossip from their front stoops. When David paused outside Elizabeth's door, one of the women looked over at him.

"You looking for someone?"

David took a chance that Euan would be going by his own name, even if Elizabeth was not.

"Mr. MacLennan," he said. "He's an old friend."

"Oh, you're Scotch, like them," the other woman said then, smiling. "Well, Mr. Mac'll be at his work, I'd think, but his missus'll be in, I reckon." She turned aside, satisfied now that she knew his business, and David knocked on the door, hoping they were right and that Elizabeth was in.

She was. She answered the door, looking pink-cheeked and dishevelled with floury hands and a tendril of dark hair stuck to her cheek.

For a long moment she just stared at David in utter disbelief, then she let out a cry and threw herself into his arms. He laughed, purely in surprise, then patted her back awkwardly. Despite everything, they had always been physically formal with one another, and this unbridled affection was entirely new.

Eventually, Elizabeth pulled back, and he saw that her eyes were wet and the hand that covered her mouth trembled.

"David—" she whispered. "It's really you."

"It is," he said, smiling. "May I come in?"

She laughed at that, through her tears, a lovely happy sound that made him feel good. "Of course, what am I thinking? Come in, come in!"

She ushered him into a tiny hallway, closing the door behind them.

"You look well," she said, looking him over. Her roving gaze snagged on his cane, and she added, "Did you walk here?"

"All the way from Mayfair."

"Mayfair? Goodness me, that's miles!"

"Yes, well, my knee's grumbling a bit now," David admitted. "Do you suppose I could sit down?"

"Of course! Look at me, keeping you standing here! Come into the kitchen and sit down. I'm making a pie."

She bustled in front of him, and he noticed she'd put a little weight on. She was, once again, the round, cheerful girl he'd first known, rather than the thin, haunted one who had returned to Edinburgh after months of marriage to Sir Alasdair Kinnell. Now, in a plain, green-and-white gown with a serviceable apron over it, she looked very far from that sad, wealthy and finely dressed woman.

"You're making a pie?" David repeated, following her into the kitchen, a small, cosy room, with a good-going fire in the hearth. "I didn't even know you could cook."

He sat on one of the mismatched chairs grouped round the table in the middle of the room. It was a rough-hewn old thing, but the edges of the wood were worn soft by years of use, and he eased into it thankfully, biting back the sigh of relief that wanted to emerge as he took the weight off his leg.

"I couldn't cook before," Elizabeth admitted. "But of course, I'm having to learn. I've been making lots of mistakes, but I think I'm getting the hang of it now." She dipped her hand into a can of flour and dusted the wooden table with her bounty. The gesture—ordinary, domestic—reminded David sharply of sitting at his mother's table when he was a child, and he felt a sudden wave of nostalgia for those simple, uncomplicated times.

"At any rate," Elizabeth went on, blushing faintly,

eyes fixed on the floury wood, "Euan thinks my apple pie is wonderful."

David watched her, touched by her quietly defiant embarrassment.

"Is he working just now?" he asked, more to put her at ease than to ask a question to which he could already guess the answer.

She looked up then and smiled gratefully. "Yes, but he'll be back later, for dinner. You'll stay for dinner, David? He'll want to see you, of course."

"I'd love to," he assured her. The longer he was away from Murdo right now, the better.

"Good," she said and bustled away to fetch something out of the larder.

David knew that now was the time to speak, now the time to tell her about her father. He knew he ought not to delay further, but it was difficult to find the words, and he couldn't say them to the back of her head.

She emerged from the larder with a bowl of pastry dough in her hands and began rolling it into a wide, flat circle with a wooden pin, chattering about her cooking adventures. David smiled and nodded, watching her turn the pastry and flour it, all the while steeling himself to speak the words that wouldn't come.

Once Elizabeth was satisfied with the shape of her rolled-out dough, she curled the flattened disc round her wooden pin and carefully draped it over a dish of cut-up apples that was waiting on the table. The thin pastry settled over the bumpy fruit like a bed sheet, and she nicked a hole in the middle of it before trimming the excess pastry away and pinching the edges closed, her actions deft and sure.

"You look quite the thing," David said. "I'd've thought you'd been cooking for years if I didn't know otherwise."

"Apple pie is simple," Elizabeth said, taking the lid off a huge cast-iron pot and carefully placing the pie dish inside.

David recognised the pot as being very like one his mother used for baking, and just as his mother did at home, Elizabeth used a stout stick to pick up the pot and hoist it onto the fire, covering the lid with a few shovelfuls of hot embers, so that the pie inside was surrounded by heat.

"Let's have a cup of tea while we wait," she said, adding after a long pause, "It's so very good to see you, David."

"It's good to see you too," he said honestly. All these months, he'd worried about her, haunted by the memory of how she'd changed following her marriage. And here she was—quite restored to her old self, wonderfully resilient. The only thing that weighed on him now was the knowledge of what he had to tell her. He took a deep breath.

"Elizabeth. I'm afraid I—"

"Wait—" she interrupted hastily. "Let me get the tea on, and then you can tell me anything you like." She smiled, her voice almost too bright, and turned away to lift a kettle over the fire and fetch a teapot and small wooden box down from the mantel.

"This is my luxury," she confided, opening the box and carefully measuring out a small spoon of leaves. "Euan bought me half a pound of this as a little present because he knows I adore tea, and I've been eking it out for weeks. Tea's so expensive!" She was so cheerful, yet so…brittle. He looked at her properly then and saw that she was afraid. She had guessed his purpose.

"I'm honoured that you're prepared to share your treasure with me." He smiled.

It was a lighthearted comment, but it made her pause, and her voice was serious when she said, "I hope you know that there is nothing I would not share with you. How can I begin to thank you for what you did? You could have been"—her voice broke a little, and she swallowed hard—"you could have been killed. When I heard what had happened to you, I felt utterly wretched."

He didn't know what to say to that. In truth, he hadn't anticipated Elizabeth's escape would have such violent consequences, and he felt a fraud to be showered with gratitude. It wasn't as though he'd known how steep the price would be when he'd offered to help her.

"There is no need to feel wretched," he said. "I am all recovered. And now, coming here, seeing you happy and whole... Well, I am very glad to have seen that for myself."

She watched him for several long moments, and he could see she was wrestling with whatever she had to say next. When at last she spoke, her voice was little more than a whisper.

"Is that why you're here? To see how I am?"

The grief in her soft, brown gaze was terrible, but worse was the glimmer of hope.

To David's surprise, sudden tears welled in his eyes. He'd never been a man for public displays of emotion, but there was so much between them, and he'd never had to bear news like this before.

"Elizabeth—"

She sank into the chair opposite him and reached across the table for his hand. Her small fingers gripped his with surprising strength.

"You are here about my father," she said. "Is he dead?"

David made himself speak, made himself say the impossible words. "When I left him a week ago, he was hanging on, but barely. You should expect the news any day now."

Elizabeth's eyes grew glassy with tears that brimmed, trembling with the promise of their imminent fall as she absorbed David's words.

"That's not why I'm here, though," David went on. "I wasn't sent to give you that news. I was sent here to make arrangements in relation to your trust. Your uncle wrote to your father after Kinnell appeared at his office—your father was worried."

"Was he?" The tears fell then, casting down her pale cheeks. "Oh, David, I've brought him nothing but grief in his final days! Grief and shame. A runaway daughter deserting her husband."

"Don't think that!" David protested. "He was comforted to know you were away, safe from Kinnell. And I was able to promise him I would look out for you—and to tell him that Euan would protect you too. He knows you have friends who will do anything to keep you safe, and he cares nothing for your supposed shame."

"But I will never him see again," she cried. "And the last time I did see him, I said almost nothing to him. Alasdair was with me, and I was afraid to speak. His last memory of me is of a silent, frightened girl."

David squeezed her hand to make her look at him and shook his head. "He has a lifetime of memories of you, not just that one. And in these last months, he's had all your letters to show him you have recovered and grown strong and happy again. When you ran away from Kinnell, you took his greatest sorrow from his shoulders. There is nothing you could have done to make him happier."

"Do you think so?" she choked through her tears.

He raised her small hand to his cheek in an uncharacteristic show of affection. Her grief pierced his usual stiffness, made a mockery of his customary reserve.

"I know it," he said. "I know it."

Chapter Eleven

As painful as it was to give Elizabeth the news about her father, David was glad he'd been the one to do it. Glad that he'd been able to sweep her guilty regrets aside and give her the comfort that only someone who knew her father could. It had helped David too, the private sharing of grief between them subtly easing his own sorrow.

By the time Euan returned to the house at six, Elizabeth was calm again, though David thought that Euan looked strained. He entered the tiny kitchen, pulling up short in surprise when he saw David.

"Davy!"

Euan's incipient smile died on his lips as his gaze turned to Elizabeth and then down to something he held in his hand—a letter. He proffered it to Elizabeth.

"It's from your sister," he said gravely. "There was another for me"—he broke off, gaze roaming to David again—"but perhaps the news has preceded me?"

David said nothing. He didn't need to. Elizabeth

had already broken the seal on the letter and was scanning the lines. Her expression remained calm, but he guessed what the letter said from the faint rounding of her shoulders and the lowering of her head.

"He's gone," she said. "My father died on Tuesday morning."

"Oh, Lizzie—"

Euan went to her, wrapping his arms around her and kissing the top of her head, murmuring endearments and reassurances. If David had been in any doubt about what they were to one another, he could not have remained so after seeing this. He glanced away from them, touched by Euan's devotion, but also—envious. The envy was a savage, unworthy howl in his breast, and he muzzled it quickly, ruthlessly, appalled at himself.

At length they broke apart, and as Elizabeth wiped her damp cheeks, Euan took the chair beside David at the kitchen table.

"Forgive me, Davy. I've barely greeted you." He smiled a little sadly. "But it's good to see you again, and looking so well. We were so worried about you, weren't we, Lizzie?"

Elizabeth said, "I was wretched with worry when I heard you'd been hurt."

"She felt responsible for your injuries," Euan added. "And there was nothing I could say to convince her otherwise."

"You couldn't possibly have known what would happen," David said, fixing his gaze on Elizabeth. "No better than I myself did. The truth is, it was down to rotten luck more than anything—not heroics on my part."

"Don't say that!" Elizabeth protested. "I *know* what you did. Euan saw you go after Alasdair. You stopped him getting to me, and in return, he pushed you under that horse." She swallowed. "You were hurt because of me."

"Well, now I'm fine," David said. He meant to sound firm and certain. Instead he sounded surly.

Elizabeth looked at him for a long moment, her expression troubled. Then she said in a small voice, "But you have a cane now."

The observation hit him like a rock. He had become a man who walked with a cane. David Lauriston, who used to walk twenty miles in a day over the Pentland Hills without giving it a thought. Reduced to this.

He tried to hide how much her words affected him, pasting a smile on his face.

"The cane's temporary," he said. "I'm growing better every day. I'll be returning to Edinburgh soon. To my practice—" He broke off, as thoughts of Murdo—of leaving him and Laverock behind—surfaced again, making the smile on his face wither.

Elizabeth said nothing, but she watched him, her

gaze assessing.

After a brief silence, she said, "You've changed, David."

That surprised him. "Whatever do you mean?"

She shook her head, not in negation but wonderingly. "You don't seem all that pleased to be going back to work. And you've always been entirely absorbed by your work."

Had he been? *Entirely* absorbed?

"Of course I'm pleased," he retorted. "It'll be good to get back to it. All I need is a few days on my feet in court, and I'll be right as rain." He attempted a grin, but while Euan smiled back, Elizabeth still looked troubled, and he knew he hadn't convinced her.

Dinner was a pleasant, informal affair. They sat round a little kitchen table, the three of them talking easily as they ate. Elizabeth served up a tasty, if somewhat plain, stew of lamb and vegetables. It was a stretch to serve the three of them with it, but there was plenty of good bread and ale, and, afterward, the apple pie.

David was amused to see that Euan literally couldn't keep his eyes off Elizabeth. His gaze kept straying to her, even when David was talking, his handsome features softening with affection when he looked upon her. When she made a joke, their eyes met, shining at their shared humour, and whenever she went to rise to do something, to clear their plates or fetch some salt, he would leap up first, insisting on fetching and carrying the smallest items for her.

When he rose from his chair yet again, this time to clear away the remains of apple pie, Elizabeth finally said, in a voice that was one part amused, one part irritated, "For goodness sake, I'm not going to break. I'm just going to have a baby!"

The next instant, she clapped her hands over her mouth, eyes gone wide.

There was a long beat of silence.

"So," David said at last, tentatively breaking into the oppressive hush, "you're expecting a child?"

Elizabeth didn't say anything. She'd flushed a dull red and was staring at her hands, so it was left to Euan to answer him.

"Yes, we are," he said, and there was a glint of defiance in his blue gaze that just dared David to disapprove, "and we couldn't be happier about it. I might not be able to marry Lizzie before the law, but she's the wife of my heart, and our child will be loved as no child has before."

Elizabeth didn't say anything, but when she glanced at Euan, her brown eyes shone with trust, and for a heartbeat David felt another touch of that wild, howling envy.

"I don't doubt it for a moment," he said. "No child could wish for better parents."

He wanted to be happy for them, but his overwhelming feeling was one of dismay. The child would be presumed to be Kinnell's under the law and would be at risk if Kinnell ever tracked them down, adding another complication to their already complicated lives.

Finally, Elizabeth spoke. "I was so worried about what my father would think about it," she said sadly. "And now all I can think is that he'll never know."

Euan went to her, crouching beside her chair, touching her with gentle hands. Watching them, David considered how much disapproval their love—a runaway wife and her lover—would attract from the world. Not as much disapproval as he and Murdo would suffer were they ever found out, but more than ample. Realising that ignited something in David. Not envy this time, nor despair, but anger. Righteous anger, at a world that wouldn't stop prying and interfering, demanding that its unjust rules be followed.

He realised that Elizabeth needed to hear the rest of what Chalmers had said to him. And so did Euan.

"Your father wouldn't have minded," he said.

Elizabeth looked up. "David, I know you're trying to help, but—"

He interrupted her. "In fact, he *didn't* mind. He told me he suspected about you and Euan, and I can assure you, he wasn't shocked by the idea, or shamed by it."

He told them everything then—about Chalmers's suspicions that Elizabeth was growing to love Euan, and about his hopes for Elizabeth's happiness. About Mary Cunningham, the woman Chalmers had loved, and about Chalmers's own personal regrets.

He told them that Chalmers had said that love should not be denied.

It was when he spoke those words that Elizabeth began to sob. Quietly at first, but soon she was crying hard, helpless to stop herself. She turned into Euan's arms to hide her face while the grief that swamped her dragged tearing gasps from her chest.

"God, I'm so sorry," David exclaimed, appalled. "I shouldn't have spoken—"

She shook her head against Euan's chest in denial but couldn't seem to form words.

"Come on," Euan murmured into her hair. "Let's get you into bed. You're exhausted." He helped her up, one protective arm round her shoulders, and looked at David over her head. "Do you mind waiting here on your own for a little while?"

"Of course not."

"Have some ale. I'll be back."

Euan led Elizabeth out of the room and into the bedchamber next door. The house was so tiny David could still hear her ragged weeping, the sound of her sorrow interspersed with the soothing rumble of Euan's voice as he comforted her.

David sat at the little kitchen table, nursing his ale, half listening to the indistinct song of Elizabeth's grief through the wall. The worst passed, fading first to hiccoughing sobs, then to silence. Still David waited, tracing the scars on the ancient table with his fingertips and trying his best not to think of his own troubles—of Murdo and the woman he was promised to. Of the months of silence Murdo had maintained, no hint of the truth passing his lips. And of the world that would part David from Murdo anyway, when David had to return to his own life.

At last, Euan returned. He looked weary to the very bone. He took his seat at the table beside David and poured himself another glass of ale.

"How is she?" David asked.

"She's been waiting for the news about her father for weeks," he said. "She knew it was coming. But it was still a shock to her to get it."

"We never really believe it till it happens," David agreed. They drank together, a silent toast.

"I wish I'd met him," Euan said after a while. "I'd've liked to have shaken his hand, just once."

"He was a good man," David said. "You'd have liked him."

"He certainly raised his daughter to be a fine woman."

"He did that."

David glanced at the clock. It was after ten and

very dark out. "I should go." He sighed. "I meant to be away long before now. It's late."

Euan frowned. "You can't go, Davy. Stay the night. It's far too late to be out walking on your own on these streets, especially with you being a stranger to London."

David opened his mouth to protest, but then he remembered how long the walk here had been. He wasn't sure he could bear it all the way back, not with his leg aching as it was now, and Euan was right about how late it was.

And then there was the fact that he didn't want to face Murdo yet.

For a moment, he hesitated, wondering if Murdo might be concerned at him not returning, but then, he reasoned, Murdo would be far more incensed at the idea of him walking through the strange dark streets on his own.

"All right," he conceded. "But where am I to sleep?"

"I'll make you up a bed in the parlour," Euan said. "Will you be all right on the floor?"

David pasted on a smile. "Of course," he lied.

At some point in the early hours, David reflected that he had grown far too used to featherbeds. All night, he tossed and turned on the floor. The hard surface was barely cushioned by the blankets Euan had laid down to form a makeshift mattress. By the time dawn broke, he felt like he'd barely slept an hour and his hip throbbed.

He was lying on his back, willing himself back to sleep, when Euan tiptoed into the parlour.

"Sorry to disturb you," Euan whispered. "I need my notebook. I'm going up to Regent's Canal to speak to some of the workers there."

"For a story?" David asked, sitting up and rubbing at his eyes.

"Yes. About the working conditions."

"Not to praise them, I take it?"

Euan's only answer was a derisive snort.

"How's *Flint's* doing?" David asked. *Flint's Political Register* was the paper Euan worked for, a radical periodical, popular amongst ordinary people and hated by the government.

"It's selling well," Euan said, "which has its drawbacks. We've not had a raid for a while, but you can't get complacent. We'll be moving the press again next month. We always have to try to stay a step ahead." Anxiety clouded his eyes. "My greatest worry is that somehow my working for *Flint's* may bring Lizzie to someone's attention. Kinnell is involved in politics—in the margins, it is true, but he is a government supporter and, as you know, our little rag has attracted some unwelcome attention from that quarter."

David sat up, frowning. "You have to be careful. You know Kinnell's already been in London looking for Elizabeth. Have you considered moving elsewhere? There are other papers. Other cities."

"I've suggested it to Lizzie already, but she didn't want me to give up *Flint's*. I think I'm going to have to insist, though, given recent events. The worry's killing me. Especially now the baby's coming."

"You should go. Elizabeth has the income from her trust that you can rely on while you find new work."

"I don't like to rely on her money."

"I thought you believed in equality between men and women," David replied.

Euan flushed at that. "That's just what Lizzie would say," he admitted. Then he looked at the clock and sighed. "I have to go, but I'm going to raise this with her again this evening. Do you think you might also mention it to her before you leave? She'll listen to you. She thinks every word that drops from your lips is perfect wisdom."

"Well, she's perfectly right, of course," David answered, smiling. Euan just rolled his eyes.

Once the other man had said his farewells and departed, David rose and put away his bed. There was no point trying to sleep any longer. He might be exhausted, but the bright morning light and the pain in his hip and leg would conspire to keep him awake.

After a perfunctory wash, he dressed. He'd removed his trousers and waistcoat before going to bed so they were in reasonable order, but it was difficult to tie his wilted neckcloth in anything but the most basic of knots.

Once dressed, he checked his appearance in a cloudy mirror over the fireplace, noting that he must've lain oddly on his pillow because his hair—his now far-too-long hair—was sticking up at an odd angle at the back. He was trying to smooth it down with water when Elizabeth entered the parlour in a plain muslin gown and her long, brown hair about her shoulders. He'd never seen her with her hair down before, and it felt uncomfortably intimate to witness this private state of being.

"Good morning," she said.

"Good morning. Are you feeling better?"

She nodded, seeming embarrassed. "I'm sorry about last night."

"Don't be. I only wish I'd considered that it might be too soon to be telling you everything your father said to me."

"It wasn't too soon," she replied. "It was exactly the right time. But I'm sorry you had to witness what came after. I made you uncomfortable."

"No, not at all. Only sorry and concerned."

"Well, there's no need for you feel either of those things." She took a deep breath, then gave a slightly forced smile. "Are you having trouble with your hair? Shall I fetch you some of Euan's pomade?"

David smiled back. "That might be wise. I look

like a hedgehog. Shall I get the range going in the meantime?"

"Would you?" She sounded grateful for the reprieve from the tedious task.

She slipped away again while David went to the kitchen and began to clear out the ashes of last night's fire, ignoring his protesting leg. This had been one of his jobs when he lived at home as a boy. First thing when he got up each morning, clearing out the kitchen fireplace for his mother. It felt strangely comforting to do it again now.

When Elizabeth came back, she'd fastened her hair in a loose knot at the back of her head and put an apron over her gown. She handed him a little blue jar, and when he pried the lid off, he was assailed by the clean, astringent scent of pine. He worked some of the paste into his hair and smoothed it down, more successfully this time, while Elizabeth put a kettle of water on the fire and began slicing bread.

She handed him a toasting fork wordlessly, and he stabbed it into a slice of bread to hold over the flames. They drew their chairs up to the fire and sat companionably, toasting their bread while the water boiled.

"Is *anything* nicer than buttered toast?" Elizabeth wondered aloud once they'd begun eating. Her chin gleamed with a sheen of melted butter and her face beamed. When David chuckled, she laughed too. "I've become very attached to toast lately," she admitted.

It was nice too, even with day-old bread and tea brewed a little too weak so as to eke the leaves out a little longer.

"What will you do today?" Elizabeth asked.

"I mean to visit your uncle," he said. "I need to speak to him about moving the trust. It was his idea, so there will be no difficulty, but I want to ask if he has any recommendations as to who else might take it on." He paused, then added, "Of course, it depends where you intend to settle. I should place it with a solicitor situated close to where you will be."

She frowned at that and looked up. "What do you mean? We are settled here."

David paused. "But is that wise?" he asked. "Kinnell has already been looking for you in London. Perhaps a fresh start in another city or town would be prudent."

"London is a big place," she said. "And just because Alasdair tracked down Uncle Charles doesn't mean he knows anything of my whereabouts. He could simply have discovered the family connection. It wouldn't be difficult. I've not been back to Uncle Charles's offices since he wrote to me to warn me to stay away, and once you've moved the trust to a solicitor unconnected to me, that should be the last of the matter."

Frowning, David said, "He's not going to stop looking for you. Having discovered your uncle, he might easily intensify his efforts in London. It's much less likely that he'd think to try Bristol or York or Manchester."

Elizabeth sighed. "I suppose so. But Euan is so well established at *Flint's*—"

"He doesn't mind leaving it, though, does he? He told me that he's already suggested you go elsewhere."

"I know, but I don't want him to give up his position over me! He's making a name for himself—well, a pen name. He doesn't dare use his own." She huffed out a laugh at that, though it didn't contain much humour.

"Listen," David said, leaning forward over the table. He put a hand over hers. "Your father placed a generous capital sum in trust for you. Properly managed, the income from it will give you a small, steady income, enough to live on—not in luxury but certainly very respectably. If Euan is willing to leave his position behind and look for another elsewhere—well, I think you should thank your lucky stars and go along with it. Go somewhere Kinnell would never think to look, somewhere there is no chance of you ever meeting anyone you've been introduced to before—one of the big industrial cities. That's where Euan's kind of stories are anyway."

She paused, considering. "I'll think about it," she said at last.

"Do that," David replied and said no more. He'd planted the seed. It would have to be enough for now.

Once they'd finished their breakfast, David rose from his chair.

"I should go," he said. "Murdo will be wondering where I've got to."

She glanced at him. "Lord Murdo is with you?"

"He was coming to London already. I just begged a seat in his carriage."

"And you're staying with him while you're here?"

"Yes, at his house on Curzon Street."

A pause. "Lord Murdo has been very kind to you. Taking you to his estate to recuperate. And now this. You have become friends, then?"

David smiled, but he could feel how tight and unnatural it must look. "I suppose we have," he admitted.

"Was he expecting you to return last night? Will he be worried?"

David considered how to answer that. Was it credible that a man who merely regarded David as a friend would worry about him if he stayed away for a night? "He knew I was coming to see you," he said at last, his voice deliberately casual. "So I'm sure he'll have realised I stayed the night here. After all, I didn't set out until quite late. All the same, I should go back and offer my apologies—once I've seen your uncle, of course. His office is quite close to here, is it not?"

Elizabeth nodded. "At Serjeant's Inn. It's perhaps a mile from here and on your way back to Curzon Street.

I'll write the directions down for you."

She rose from her chair to attend to her task, thoroughly diverted from her curiosity about Murdo Balfour.

Chapter Twelve

Charles Carr's offices were compact but well appointed. There were two rooms, Mr. Carr's own office—the door to which was presently closed—and a sizeable anteroom which accommodated two clerks and several commodious chairs where clients waiting to see Mr. Carr could make themselves comfortable.

Having announced himself, David was invited to sit by one of the clerks who slipped off his tall stool, presumably to advise Mr. Carr of David's arrival. On his return, the clerk retreated behind his desk to continue with his work, and the only sounds to disturb the silence for the next quarter hour were the scratches of nibs on paper.

At length, Mr. Carr's door opened, and two people emerged, a neat, white-haired man wearing spectacles and an even smaller elderly lady who held his arm tightly. As the man, whom David presumed was Mr. Carr, led his elderly charge towards the front door, he nodded at David and said, "I will be with you once I've escorted Mrs. Kirkton to her carriage, Mr. Lauriston."

"Please take your time," David replied, nodding in return.

It was a full ten minutes before Mr. Carr returned.

He paused beside David's chair. "Would you care to join me in my office, Mr. Lauriston?"

"Yes, of course." David grasped his cane, wincing a little as he rose from his chair, a detail that he was quite sure the watchful solicitor noted.

As they passed the clerk on his high stool, Mr. Carr paused, saying, "Will you ask Polly to bring some tea in to us, Mr. Jenkins?"

The clerk murmured his assent, and Mr. Carr ushered David into his office.

It was a large, comfortably furnished room, reassuring in its solidity. The dark wood of the sizeable mahogany desk gleamed with care, and the hundreds of books that lined the walls looked to be regularly dusted. The desk itself was entirely clear, except for one small, tidy pile of papers right in the middle, tied up neatly with pink ribbon. Mr. Carr lifted the little bundle and placed it in a wooden tray that occupied a corner of the desk. Then he sat down, gesturing at David to take the chair on the other side of the desk.

"I've been expecting you, Mr. Lauriston," he said. "You or Mr. Ferguson, anyway."

"I hope you don't mind me coming without an appointment," David replied. "I only arrived in town late yesterday afternoon. If now is inconvenient…"

He trailed off as Mr. Carr shook his head. "Not at all," the older man said. He paused, then added, "Before we go further, I should ask if you've heard about Patrick."

"That he's passed away?" David felt the heaviness of his sorrow again as he nodded. "Yes. I went to see Elizabeth yesterday, and a letter came from her sister with the news."

Mr. Carr nodded. "He is a great loss to his family and to the legal profession. A fine man."

"The finest," David whispered.

"He had a very high regard for you, Mr. Lauriston."

David couldn't speak in response to that, and perhaps Mr. Carr saw it, because he became suddenly businesslike.

"Now, as to Miss Elizabeth, our beneficiary. I assume you are aware of what happened recently?"

David nodded. "I know that Sir Alasdair came here, seeking information as to her whereabouts. In the circumstances, I understand you advised Mr. Chalmers that it would be prudent to move the administration of the trust to another solicitor."

"That is correct, so far as it goes," Mr. Carr said. "Though there is a little more to the story than I wished to share by letter with my poor brother-in-law." He leaned forward and took hold of a small bell. It gave only a light tinkle, but a moment later the door opened and the clerk who had greeted David on his arrival peered inside.

"Yes, sir?"

"Would you kindly arrange for Mrs. Kirkton's papers to be returned to storage, Mr. Jenkins? No change to the current arrangements required. Just a little chat today."

The clerk approached the desk and lifted the bundle of neatly tied papers out of the wooden tray. "Very good, sir."

"Thank you."

As the clerk left, closing the door quietly behind him, Mr. Carr returned his calm gaze to David.

"This office is rather small, Mr. Lauriston, so we store most of our clients' files and papers in another location close by. The clerks fetch what I need and return it when I'm done. In all, they make several journeys each day."

Puzzled, David nodded. "That sounds sensible," he agreed.

"Sensible and…fortunate."

"Fortunate?"

"As I said, I didn't tell Patrick the whole story of Sir Alasdair's visit here. He came in the afternoon. The same night, this office was broken into and turned upside down. There were a few client papers on my desk, but only what I'd been working on that day. Nothing pertaining to Elizabeth's trust. Nothing that would reveal her whereabouts."

David stared at the other man, at his tidy, polite countenance, and didn't know what to say for a moment. "You think Kinnell—" he began, breaking off in sheer disbelief.

"Candidly?" Mr. Carr said. "I do. I can prove nothing, of course. But Sir Alasdair made it fairly clear to me during our—quite unpleasant—conversation that he believed I had knowledge of Elizabeth's whereabouts, and if I wasn't prepared to tell him, he would take whatever action was necessary to find out for himself."

A soft knock on the door interrupted them.

"Come in," Mr. Carr said.

A middle-aged maidservant bearing a tea tray entered. She set it down on the large desk and bobbed a curtsey.

"Thank you, Polly," Mr. Carr said in his calm, pleasant voice. "Those biscuits look delicious, I must say."

The maidservant beamed and departed.

David found himself smiling too. Mr. Carr's scrupulous politeness appeared to extend not only to his clients and visitors, but to his clerks and servants. Now the man was pouring a cup of tea for David, adding a splash of milk and offering him a plate of biscuits that looked to be freshly baked. David took one and bit into it. It was every bit as delicious as Mr. Carr thought, a crispy little wafer of sugar that melted in the mouth.

"What else did Kinnell say when he was here?" David asked.

Mr. Carr sat back in his chair, folding his hands over his chest. "Let me see. Well, when he first arrived, I was with another client—as I was when you arrived this morning. Sir Alasdair wasn't as content as yourself to wait. He made such a racket that I had no choice but to excuse myself to my client and go out to investigate what the hullabaloo was. When I emerged from my office, he announced loudly that he knew who I was and he'd thank me to tell him where his wife was before he was forced to knock my teeth down my throat."

"Charming."

"Isn't he? I told him I had no idea what he was talking about, but if he'd care to explain, I was happy to listen. That prompted him to tell me that I was as bad as his father-in-law."

"Compliments, then?"

Mr. Carr gave a chuckle, but then he sighed. "He was not merely guessing, Mr. Lauriston. He *knows* she is here, in the city. He does not know where, but he knows."

"How?"

"I don't know. But I could see there was no doubt in his mind about it. He was by no means sure of my involvement, but he was sure about that."

"I've told her she should leave London. There are many other cities she could easily disappear in."

"I couldn't agree more. We were lucky there were no trust papers here when Sir Alasdair sent his men. Her address is recorded in the files. The papers are being kept safely with my bankers now, but you should identify a new solicitor to deal with the trust, someone with no connection to her."

"I will do so. But Elizabeth needs to decide where she's going first."

"She does," Mr. Carr agreed. "And the sooner she leaves London, the better."

Mr. Liddle answered the door when David knocked on the front door of the Curzon Street house an hour later.

"Good afternoon, sir," the butler said, holding the door open. "His Lordship is in his study. Shall I show you through?"

"I think I'll go to my bedchamber first, thank you," David said, but when he went to move toward the stairs, the butler placed an impertinent hand on his forearm.

"I believe His Lordship would appreciate it if you would let him know that you are back, sir," he said quietly. "He was a little concerned when you did not return last night."

"Oh," David said, mortified at being so softly rebuked. He'd rather hoped to wash up and put on clean clothes before confronting Murdo, but if Murdo had been worried about him, he supposed he should show face as early as possible. "All right, then."

Abandoning the stairs, he followed Liddle along the corridor, past the drawing room and on to another door that presumably led to Murdo's study.

The butler knocked softly at the door, but there was no answer. He knocked again, a little louder this time.

"I beg your pardon, sir," he said to David over his shoulder. "Perhaps His Lordship has returned to his own rooms." Having delivered that pronouncement, he opened the door, only to halt in the doorway—David behind him—when he saw that room was, in fact, occupied. Murdo half reclined in the large chair behind the desk, eyes closed and head lolling on his shoulder. He was asleep, and given that he still wore the clothes he'd been in when David left him yesterday, perhaps that wasn't a surprise. Had he waited up for David all night?

David glanced at the butler, who seemed suddenly paralysed by indecision.

"Leave us, please, Mr. Liddle." When the butler opened his mouth to protest, David cut him off before he could speak. "I will take responsibility."

The butler didn't look particularly reassured by that comment, but he gave a stiff bow and withdrew, closing the study door quietly behind himself. David crossed the room, glad of the rug below his feet that muffled his steps. He stopped in front of Murdo's chair and gazed down at his lover. The other man looked exhausted and rumpled. Utterly done in. It was close to noon now, and David found himself wondering how long Murdo had been sleeping. If his drawn, pale face was anything to go by, it hadn't been long.

Staring down at Murdo, knowing that his lover had been worried about him, David felt a pang of guilt—and something else too. A bewildered sort of tenderness, an odd protectiveness that made him reluctant to wake the other man.

David rarely saw Murdo like this, quiet and passive. When they were in bed, Murdo took charge. He was naturally assertive, and since David preferred to cede control, they had fallen into a rhythm that suited both of them. It was easy to forget that Murdo was as breakable as anyone else. Seeing him like this now, tired and vulnerable, was a reminder of that.

The odd spell that held David locked in place was broken when Murdo began to stir. His wakening began with a soft moan and a series of tiny shifts of his body, until he finally lifted his head and, with a slow blink, opened his eyes.

"David," he breathed, smiling. Then, as memory returned, he sat up abruptly in his chair, demanding in a rusty, too-loud voice, "Where the *hell* have you been?"

David had to suppress an urge to snap back in the face of that aggression, answering calmly, "I stayed the night with Euan and Elizabeth. It seemed a better option than walking home in the pitch-dark."

"You stayed the night!" Murdo exclaimed. "Didn't it occur to you to at least let me know you were safe?"

"And how was I supposed to do that?" David asked, his own voice rising now.

"A dozen ways. You could've sent a note."

David gave a disbelieving laugh. "By whose hand? Euan and Elizabeth don't have a retinue of servants like you, you know. They don't even have *one* servant!"

"I'm sure you could've found someone who'd've been willing to bring me a note for a coin or two," Murdo snapped. Then he sighed, and the anger seemed to go out of him. He rubbed his hands over his unshaven cheeks in a weary motion.

"I'm sorry," he added more quietly. "I was worried."

David leaned back against the edge of the desk, the better to look Murdo in the eye. It seemed, though, that the other man wasn't for meeting David's gaze. He stared at the shiny mahogany surface of the desk as though fascinated by it, a faint flush heating his high cheekbones.

"You knew I was with friends," David said carefully. "I told you where I was going. And it's not so very surprising I didn't come back, given the lateness of the hour, is it? Would you have preferred me to walk home in the dark?"

Murdo shook his head. "You misunderstand me. I was worried something may have befallen you on the way."

"Well, that's just silly. It was still light when I set off." David gave a soft chuckle, but it died in his throat when he saw the expression on Murdo's face and realised he was perfectly serious.

"I was worried that my father may have arranged for someone to follow you," Murdo said. "It didn't occur to me till after you left, but once I thought of it, I couldn't stop. I was convinced you were lying, beaten, in some alleyway."

"What? He wouldn't do that, would he?"

Murdo considered, his brows drawn together. "I just don't know," he said after a long pause. "But then I didn't think he even knew about you—until he came here yesterday and made it clear he was well aware I had someone staying with me at Laverock House." He shook his head, lips thinning. "Which means that someone's been sending him reports—just when I thought I'd weeded all of that out."

"But why go to the bother of setting someone on my heels? What does that achieve?"

"To get you out the way," Murdo said flatly. "You're an obstacle to his plans. And I feel like the worst sort of fool because I'm the one who made him see it."

David swallowed, his gut clenching with nerves. "How do you think you managed that?"

"For months I've been ignoring his demands to return to London to get married. Ignoring him is how I deal with him, you see. I realised long ago that it's a mistake to fall into the trap of providing explanations for not doing what he wants. Refusing to speak to him is so much more effective and satisfying. Unfortunately, I made an error of judgment when he came here yesterday."

"What error?"

"I should have sat back and waited for him to play his hand. He'd've revealed that he knew about you eventually, if I'd been patient. Instead, I jumped in with both feet. Told him straight off that I wouldn't be going through with the wedding. I thought you were asleep upstairs and that he was entirely unaware of your existence. But just before you came down, he asked whether my decision was something to do with the man I'd had living with me for the last six months." Murdo paused, then added, "And then you arrived."

David closed his eyes. "Damn. I'm sorry."

"Don't be. It was my stupid fault. If I'd done what I usually do—just listened to whatever he had to say without blurting out my own thoughts—I'd've got a hint from him eventually that he knew about you, and that would have changed everything." He looked up at

David, his gaze pleading. "But for once, I didn't have the patience for his games—I just wanted to get it over with. End it. Go and see Lord Hartley and negotiate the compensation and the terms of the announcement." He swallowed. "I couldn't think of anything but getting the whole thing over with as soon as possible so I could tell you, at last, and we could go home to Laverock."

Home.

Murdo's face was grey with exhaustion and despair, every line of his big body tense. He rubbed his whiskery face with his big hands while David watched and wondered what to say. The anger that had sent David stalking off to Blackfriars yesterday was already slipping from his grasp, despite the nagging feeling he ought not to let it go.

Was he a fool to think about forgiving Murdo for keeping his engagement a secret? Or was Murdo's secrecy understandable? He couldn't decide what was the more reasonable position, and the more he thought about it, the more he realised that he felt as tired as Murdo looked.

Well, perhaps he didn't need to decide. Not now. Perhaps that could wait till more immediate concerns were taken care of.

He reached out his hand to Murdo.

"You've barely slept these last few days," he murmured. "And I'm not doing much better. There's no sense hashing this out now. Let's go to bed and get some sleep. We can talk about things properly when we're less exhausted."

Murdo looked up at him, his expression defeated. "How can I go to bed, David? I've put you in danger. We need to talk about how we're going to keep you safe. I don't—"

"Later," David interrupted firmly. "We can talk about all of that tonight. For now, you need to sleep. And in truth, so do I. I was on Euan and Elizabeth's floor last night, and my hip ached so badly I barely slept an hour." He gave a lopsided smile.

Murdo didn't say anything for a moment. Then he sighed, stood up and set his hand in David's. "Provided you come with me," he said, "I won't argue."

Chapter Thirteen

When David awoke, it was late afternoon. He'd slept nearly four hours, dead to the world from the moment his head touched the pillow. Four hours probably shouldn't have been enough to make up for two nights of missed sleep, but somehow it was. He felt refreshed and alert.

He shifted onto his side to look at Murdo, who was sleeping on his front, his face hidden in the crook of one burly arm. David smoothed his hand over Murdo's almost-black hair, enjoying the soft feel of it below his fingers.

"Hmmm."

He drew back at Murdo's moan of pleasure, not wanting to wake him, but it was too late. Murdo stirred and, a moment later, turned over to smile lazily at David.

"Hello," he murmured.

"I didn't mean to wake you," David whispered. "Go back to sleep."

Murdo just chuckled softly, shifting himself onto

his side so that they faced one another. He touched David's cheek, then let his fingertips drift down, exploring David's raspy jawline before moving down the column of his throat. The caress was a mere whisper, making David shiver, gooseflesh rising.

"I need to kiss you," Murdo murmured. "It feels like forever since I kissed you." He closed the remaining space between them, the warm, naked length of his body brushing David's. His smile was warm and intimate, affectionate. David could feel the curve of it when Murdo pressed their lips together, and he darted out the tip of his tongue to taste it, to taste that smile and to know it. Their noses brushed in welcome, cheeks skimming as they deepened the kiss. Warm skin met warm skin and firm, muscled limbs tangled, and already they were beyond mere kisses, sliding into the heady rhythm of lovemaking as easily as two dancers taking the floor at a ball.

Making love with Murdo had become vital to David over these last months. Not just for the pleasure of it but for the give and take of it, the generosity and the joy of it. These were the things that showed David that, whatever he may have once thought, he wasn't a criminal. Or a sinner. Making love with Murdo had turned David's most shameful secret into his greatest joy.

Now that give and take, that push and pull, became a lusty sort of wrestling, a brief and delicious scuffle for dominance that ended when Murdo rolled on top of David, besting him with his greater strength even as he kept his weight carefully from David's injured leg. Murdo grinned down at David, his wide smile denting his cheek with a deep dimple. He looked carefree and happy, and David wanted him to look like this always. His heart swelled with love and longing, and he put a hand to Murdo's cheek.

"I don't want you to marry Lady Louisa," he blurted. "I want you all to myself."

It was a painful admission, and he knew his expression must betray his agony to Murdo. Saying aloud, at last, what he wanted—desperately wanted—and knowing he couldn't have it. Knowing that his old life in Edinburgh beckoned, and that these were the last days of the happiest time of his life.

Murdo's gaze travelled over David's face as though he was measuring the words, or perhaps the sentiments behind them. His carefree smile ebbed, but his dark gaze glowed with what looked like satisfaction.

"I'm not going to marry her," he said fiercely. "I'm not going to marry anyone."

He leaned down and captured David's lips with his own.

David welcomed him, thrusting aside all thoughts of the future. All that mattered right now was this. He slid his hands over Murdo's big, warm body, loving every familiar line and curve. His cock was hard against

Murdo's thigh, a physical expression of his delight in his lover.

Murdo caged David's body with his own, carefully keeping his weight off David's injured leg. They ground together, kissing all the while, the slip and drag of flesh on flesh a madness and a joy.

"I want you inside me," Murdo murmured against David's lips.

David hesitated. They'd only tried this once before, and it hadn't been a resounding success. Murdo had traumatic memories that made it difficult for him to allow a man to penetrate him, but he'd wanted to try with David, and whilst he'd borne the experience without apparent trauma, David had been able to tell he hadn't enjoyed it much.

"You don't have to do that," he murmured back. "You prefer it the other way, and I'm perfectly happy with that."

Murdo levered himself up to look at David properly. "I want to try it again. I didn't like not being able to see you last time—and I could tell you were uncomfortable too."

A huff of laughter escaped David at that. He'd taken Murdo from behind, both of them on their knees, and despite the feather mattress, his hip and leg had ached like the very devil all the way through. "I thought I'd hidden that," he said ruefully.

"Not really." Murdo smiled. "We didn't think it

through properly, did we?"

"No. And you didn't let me prepare you properly." It amused David to see Murdo flush at that. When it came to tending to David, the man was utterly shameless, yet he'd been shy of David doing the same for him, insisting on preparing himself. "If we're trying this again, you have to let me ready you. And how are we going to deal with my leg?"

"I'll straddle you," Murdo said promptly, betraying that he'd given this some thought already. "That way, I won't feel out of control, and your leg won't get tired."

David gave a low moan. The thought of Murdo slowly impaling himself on David's cock went straight to some deep-lurking and primitive part of him that secretly wanted to fuck the whole world. His reaction elicited a smile of amused pleasure from Murdo.

"You like the idea?"

"God, yes, but are you sure? It's not easy to take a man like that, and you've not had much practice lately."

"I'm sure. We'll use lots of oil." With that, Murdo scrambled off the bed to fetch the bottle from the armoire drawer.

David slid up the bed, wedging a pillow behind his neck so he could lounge against the headboard.

When Murdo returned, he handed the bottle to David, then eyed him uncertainly. "How shall I—" He broke off and gestured vaguely at the bed.

"It would be easiest for me if you knelt over me, facing the other way," David said. When Murdo's face reddened, he couldn't resist adding with a grin, "Hips nice and high. Buttocks splayed."

Murdo's face burned. He gave a half laugh, but it was strangled with an overlay of mortification. "I don't think I can do that. Can't I just—"

"Come on," David interrupted, more gently. "Let me—I want to. You've done it to me plenty of times. It's only fair."

For a long moment, Murdo stood there, undecided. Then he gave a sigh. "Fine," he said, climbing onto the bed, his left knee brushing David's chest as he got himself into the suggested position.

And ah, but he was a fine specimen, with those firm buttocks and muscular, meaty thighs. Christ above, what a sight.

David set the bottle of oil down at his hip and skimmed his hands up the backs of Murdo's thighs, drawing a faint moan from the other man. Murdo's skin was still sleep warm and dusted with hair that rasped pleasurably against David's fingertips. Mouth dry with anticipation, he circled his palms over the firm globes of Murdo's arse, urging his hips a little higher to reveal the entrance to his body. Murdo shifted, allowing it, but the sound that fell from his lips as he did so was as much protest as pleasure.

Such a vulnerable position, this. For anyone, but

for Murdo especially, who'd been unable to allow it for so very long. Now that he was letting David see him like this, touch him like this, David had to make it pleasurable for him. Had to make Murdo's gesture of trust worthwhile.

He tugged gently at Murdo's hips, shifting his own body till he was close enough to lay a kiss upon his lover. He didn't do it yet, though, merely huffed a hot breath into the tender groove between his buttocks, making Murdo shiver and moan, still with that note of uneasy protest in his voice.

Patience, then. He would begin somewhere less provocative.

David dipped his head lower, laying a trail of kisses from the tops of Murdo's thighs to the lower curves of his buttocks then moving down to map the patch of taut flesh that led to his balls. He lavished attention there, loving the hoarse cry he finally drew from Murdo's throat, and the deep groan that emerged when David suckled his ballocks. Neglecting his own iron-hard prick, he lavished attention on Murdo's, squeezing his shaft with one hand while he mouthed the prickly purse of his scrotum, and soon enough every bit of Murdo's awkwardness had fled. His head was down, hips tipping up higher, knees splaying a little more as he spilled cries of muffled pleasure into the bedsheets.

Only then did David allow the kiss to become

more intimate, drawing his tongue up again, all the way up this time to trace the outer edge of the crevice between Murdo's buttocks. And this time, Murdo's answering cry held no protest, only desperation for more, then gratitude—"God, yes, please!"—as David went deeper.

Murdo's scent, earthy and male, was intoxicating. David held his lover open and lapped at the pinched edges of his hole, loosening and stimulating and downright worshipping. The near sobs of pleasure that guttered from the other man's lips drove him on, the thought of bringing Murdo to his crisis like this consuming him. At last, though, he forced himself to draw back. Murdo was wide open now, open and ready.

"Christ," Murdo whispered. "I need you to fuck me. Now." He went to shift, to turn around, but David stopped him with firm hands.

"Not yet."

David fumbled around for the bottle of oil, unstoppering it quickly and drizzling a thin, jewel-bright stream over Murdo's hole. Setting the bottle aside, he gathered up the dripping oil in his fingers and began to probe the muscle he'd already loosened with kisses, until he was able to slide his finger inside. Murdo's body gripped him, sucking him deeper, and both of them moaned. David's cock was so hard it ached. Watching Murdo go from tight and embarrassed to loose and aroused, watching his own fingers effortlessly fuck in and out of Murdo's body, then, even better, witnessing Murdo jerk and curse when David crooked his fingers and found the target he'd been seeking—it was enough that David was sure he could come without a single touch to his own cock. Just wringing a climax from Murdo would do it.

Another time. This time, Murdo wanted to be fucked.

"You're ready now," David said. "You can turn round."

Murdo's face, when he turned, was still flushed, but with lust now, rather than mortification. His eyes glittered like jet under half-lowered lids. He looked loose and debauched and very intent.

"I'm not going to last long," he said as he settled himself over David, raising himself up on his knees as he sought to align his hole with David's stiff mast.

"Nor am I," David gritted out, hissing as Murdo finally touched his now-weeping cock. And then Murdo was sliding down, impaling himself, his body gripping David's shaft with slick, living heat.

Oh Christ, and now David remembered this feeling from last time, only this was so much better, because this time Murdo was loving it too, his big chest heaving with effort, even as his eyes closed and his head dropped back in ecstasy. He planted one hand on the pillow, raising his hips high, then pressing them all the way down again in impossibly long, impossibly slow strokes, wrenching a series of groans from David's throat.

Murdo's prick bobbed between them, a sight that made David's mouth water. He reached for it with a hand that was still slick with oil.

"God, yes!" Murdo gasped as David closed his fist around him and began to work his hand in rhythm with Murdo's hips. "I'm so close—"

"Come on me," David muttered. "I want you to mark me."

Murdo groaned at those words, rearing back, and David felt the big shaft in his hand swell an impossible fraction more. And then Murdo's seed was pulsing out, coating his hand, and Murdo's body was gripping his cock, yanking a climax from David that had his back bowing and hips lifting from the bed.

When it was over, when Murdo had collapsed on top of him and the muffled haze of pleasure had cleared enough that David could open his eyes and actually think, he gave a soft huff of laughter, his breath gusting against Murdo's neck.

"Christ," the other man said wonderingly.

"Just what I was thinking."

"I should let you fuck me more often."

They both laughed at that, and Murdo lifted his head to look down at David. His dark eyes danced with affection and growing pleasure as he read David's own expression, which David knew must mirror Murdo's, since he was making no attempt to hide his feelings. They watched each other like that for a long time, till the joyful expression on Murdo's face softened into something more reflective, almost poignant.

"I didn't know I wasn't happy before," he murmured.

"Before what?"

Murdo gave a lopsided smile. "Before you. Not that I was actively *unhappy*. I had plans. Objectives. Things to acquire or achieve. But—" He paused, then said simply, "You make me happy, David."

David stared at him, his throat clogged with emotion. "The feeling's mutual," he managed at last, his voice little more than a whisper. Then he pulled Murdo down, pressing their lips together in a fierce kiss.

Chapter Fourteen

They dined early, neither of them having eaten much since the day before. Murdo instructed the meal to be served in his private sitting room, which meant they could sit down in their shirtsleeves and rest their elbows on the small table, eating from each other's plates with impunity. While they ate, David told Murdo about his visit to Elizabeth and Euan, and his subsequent interview with Mr. Carr.

Murdo frowned when he was finished. "I don't like the thought of you being mixed up in all this again. Kinnell already bears a grudge against you, and he's a vindictive bastard. In all likelihood, the only reason he's left you alone since the accident is that he knows he was lucky not to be prosecuted for what he did. If he suspects you're assisting Elizabeth, he may come after you."

David considered that. He hadn't pushed for a prosecution after the accident, thinking it best to leave well alone for Elizabeth's sake. Now that he knew Kinnell was trying to track her down, David wondered if he ought to have done so. It would be unusual for an aristocrat to face punishment for assaulting a man so far beneath him, but in this case, the incident had been witnessed by dozens of other people, including, of course, Lord Murdo Balfour, another peer of the realm, whose word would carry just as much clout as Sir Alasdair Kinnell's.

Perhaps he could make the complaint now?

Even as the thought occurred to David, he rejected it. He'd waited far too long, and even if he had not, it would be imprudent to bring his association with Murdo under scrutiny.

"Don't worry," he said now, touching Murdo's wrist. "I'll stay well away from Kinnell and leave protecting Elizabeth to Euan. All I have to do is move the administration of the trust to another solicitor, and that shouldn't take long at all—I can make the arrangements as soon as I know where Elizabeth and Euan plan to settle. Though I may have to beg the use of your carriage again to do so."

"Where are they thinking of going?"

"Somewhere industrial, I'd imagine, somewhere Kinnell would have little reason to go. Birmingham, perhaps, or Manchester."

"That'll be quite a journey," Murdo said. "You can have the carriage, of course, but you'll have to put up with my company if you're going anywhere. I have no intention of letting you out of my sight anytime soon."

"You have your own problems to resolve," David pointed out.

"And resolve them I will," Murdo assured him. "But I won't make the mistake of leaving you alone. You have a tendency to run into trouble when left to your own devices. Don't fight me on this, David."

Murdo's overbearing protectiveness didn't sit well with David. He opened his mouth to protest, but before he could do so, there was a knock at the door. It was Mr. Liddle.

"There's a gentleman asking for Mr. Lauriston," the man said. "A Mr. MacLennan."

"Euan?" David looked up, concerned. Why would Euan come here? "Where is he?"

"In the drawing room, sir," Mr. Liddle said. "I should say that he seems very agitated. He was most adamant that he speak to you straight away."

David stood up quickly, forgetting about his leg, as he occasionally did. He gave an impatient wince at the jarring pain that accompanied his precipitous action and turned to Murdo, who was also on his feet.

"Something's wrong, isn't it?" Murdo said.

"I can't think why else he'd come here," David admitted.

Euan was pacing the floor when they entered the drawing room. He turned at their entrance, and his face was a mask of grief.

"Davy," he said, "Kinnell's taken Lizzie. His men

came for her after you left, and I wasn't there to stop them. I don't know what to do!"

"Christ, no," David said, his heart plummeting.

"He's had her for hours now and—" Euan broke off, turning away as a harsh sob tore from his chest.

David went to him, placing a hand on his shoulder. "We'll get her back," he said firmly, forcing a note of confidence into his voice that in truth he didn't feel.

"Why don't you tell us what happened?" Murdo said, making Euan look up and seem to notice him for the first time. Euan stared at Murdo for a long beat and David wondered if he was remembering the last time he'd encountered the other man—the wariness and desperation in his gaze suggested he might be.

"I hardly know anything," Euan said at last. "I came home at four o'clock, and she wasn't there. The kitchen was in a mess—she'd been cooking. I was calling her name, looking for her. That's when our neighbour Lily came round. She'd been waiting for me to come back for ages." He swallowed. "Lily saw the carriage arrive. It had to be Kinnell's; there was a crest on the door. Then she saw two men come out of the house with Lizzie between them. Servants, probably, since neither of them sounded like Kinnell. Lily said they bundled Lizzie into the carriage, and a moment later, they were gone. She was near frantic, not knowing what to do till I got back. And that's it. That's all I know." His voice was raw with pain.

"I must've led him to you," David said slowly. "I came to your house yesterday, and the very next day—God, Euan, I'm so sorry!" He felt sick inside at the thought that he was to blame for this. If only he'd been more careful, taken more precautions.

Euan just stared at him with an agonised expression, and David could see he'd reached the same conclusion.

"It's not your fault, Davy. I just—I have to get her back," Euan said. "But what the hell can I do? If Kinnell has her locked up in that house of his, I won't be able to get anywhere near her."

"To be frank," Murdo interrupted, "there's not much you can do. He's her husband, and that gives him all the power. If he gets her away from London, you'll have no chance."

"Murdo!" David hissed. Euan's face had paled at Murdo's words, and he looked like he was about to vomit.

"I'm sorry to be brutal, but we have to be realistic here," Murdo replied. "MacLennan won't be able to sort this out for himself. Only someone who moves in Kinnell's world has a chance of getting close to her now."

"Someone like you, you mean?" Euan asked.

Murdo nodded.

"And—and would you be willing to help Lizzie?" Euan asked with painful humility. "I'm not too proud to beg. I'd do anything to get her away from him. Pay you anything. Name your price."

"I don't want your money," Murdo said, sounding insulted. "I'll do what I can to help Elizabeth—for David's sake."

Euan nodded slowly, his gaze shifting between them assessingly. "All right, then," he said at last. "I—thank you. I'll take whatever help you'll give and be grateful. Do you have any ideas what to do?"

Murdo paused, considering. "I know some things about Kinnell," he said carefully. "There may be some threats I could make. I doubt Kinnell would admit me to his home, though, since he knows I'm associated with David. Which means I need to engineer a public encounter, and soon. What do you know of his habits?"

"Nothing," Euan admitted. "My first instinct was to go straight to his house—to stick a knife in the bastard, or at least see what I could find out—but I have to assume he knows about me and daresay he'd take great pleasure in setting his dogs on me. And that won't help Lizzie."

"You're right there," Murdo replied. "He'd love the chance to set his men on you. He isn't one for carrying out his own dirty work. Even when he was boy, he preferred to have his friends hold his victims down."

Murdo had been one of those victims, one of the younger boys at the school they'd both attended. David shivered to think of that.

"I'll ask Liddle," Murdo said, crossing the room to ring the servants' bell. "If anyone can find out how Kinnell spends his time, it's him."

A few minutes later, the butler entered the room. "My lord?"

"Mr. Liddle." Murdo smiled. "I need some enquiries carried out—quickly and discreetly. Do you suppose you could do the necessary?"

Liddle didn't react any differently to that pronouncement than he did to any other instruction Murdo ever gave him. Nor did he write any of what followed down or repeat any of the details back. He merely listened, nodding occasionally.

When Murdo was finished, Liddle said, "Sir Alasdair's house isn't far from here. An hour should be enough for me to get the information you seek, my lord. Shall I have some refreshments sent up while you wait?"

"Have a tray sent up for Mr. MacLennan," Murdo said without seeking Euan's opinion. "Mr. Lauriston and I have already eaten, and we will need to tidy ourselves up, so that we're ready to go out. We hope to track down Sir Alasdair tonight."

"Very good, my lord," the butler said and withdrew.

"A mere hour?" Euan said, frowning. "To find out the man's habits and report back?"

"Mr. Liddle is a quick worker. He knows practically every servant in London," Murdo said, "and is owed favours by most of them." He laid his hand on David's shoulder. "Come on. Let's make ourselves more presentable while Mr. MacLennan has something to eat."

"I don't want anything," Euan said. "How can I eat when I know what Lizzie must be going through?"

"You have to keep your strength up," Murdo said firmly. "You have to be ready to act and if you neglect yourself you'll be less able to do that. Think of Elizabeth."

"All right," Euan muttered unhappily. "I'll try."

David followed Murdo out of the drawing room and up the stairs to their respective bedchambers. Both of them were in dire need of a shave. David's sparse auburn whiskers merely looked untidy, but Murdo's dark beard grew in so quickly he looked as disreputable as a pirate.

When they reached the top of the stairs and Murdo went to turn away towards his own chamber, David detained him. "You told Euan you were helping him for my sake."

"I did."

"Why?"

Murdo gazed at him for a moment. "I knew you would do anything to help him," Murdo said. He shrugged. "And I wanted to help you."

David stared at him, unsure what to say to that, but Murdo saved him the bother of replying.

"Go to your chamber and get shaved," he said gently. "And put your best clothes on. I'm not sure where we'll end up going, and we can't have you being stopped at the door because your coat doesn't pass muster."

Less than an hour later, they were back in the drawing room. Murdo was dressed in his finest, an exquisitely pressed dark-blue coat stretched over his broad shoulders and a sapphire pin glittering in the folds of his cravat. And if David didn't look quite so splendid, he still looked very fine in his black-and-white evening clothes.

The tray of food that had been brought for Euan sat on an occasional table, barely touched. The man's stomach must be in knots as he contemplated what was happening to Elizabeth. All three of them were on edge as they waited for Liddle to bring news.

At last, the butler returned.

"Happily, Sir Alasdair's coachman was able to provide a good deal of information as regards his master's habits," the butler reported. "Apparently, he accompanies Sir Alasdair almost everywhere he goes, as Sir Alasdair dislikes riding."

"What of Lady Kinnell?" Euan said. "Any news?"

Liddle's habitually cool expression softened a little at Euan's desperation. "Very little, I'm afraid, sir. The coachman said she was being kept inside. I asked him to find out more from the indoor servants and hope to get more news later tonight."

Euan nodded stiffly.

"Tell us about Kinnell, then," Murdo said.

The butler proceeded to relay the information the coachman had given him, a rehearsal of Kinnell's days in London. Breakfast at home with the morning post, a portion of each day with his secretary, visits to his tailor and afternoon calls. And in the evenings, visits to his club—Culzeans near St. James.

"Apparently he dines at Culzeans most evenings," Liddle concluded.

"Culzeans," Murdo murmured. "I might've known."

"What do you mean?" Euan asked, looking up, his interest piqued.

"Culzeans is a private club for Scots peers and men of influence," Murdo said. "Its members collectively own most of Scotland. My father is one of the leading members. It's where all the big decisions are made, where the marriages of the great and the good are brokered."

David wondered if Murdo's own engagement had been brokered there, then tamped down that thought, asking instead, "Are you a member?"

Murdo frowned. "I used to be. I haven't crossed the threshold in over ten years, but hopefully they won't have struck me from their list. We'll soon find out." He turned to the butler again. "Mr. Liddle, have the carriage brought round. Mr. Lauriston and I are going to Culzeans."

"Very good, my lord," the butler murmured, withdrawing.

"Do you really think he'll be there tonight?" Euan asked when Liddle was gone. "He's only just got Elizabeth back today, after all."

"I don't know," Murdo said. "But what choice do we have? We have to try."

Chapter Fifteen

Culzeans, which occupied a large townhouse at the edge of St. James, oozed money. From the opulent drapes at the windows to the liveried footman standing guard at the front door, it was the very picture of a wealthy gentlemen's club.

"It's not so popular as White's or Brooks's," Murdo told David, "but a lot of eminent Scots are members—though many of them will also be members of other clubs."

"Like your father?"

Murdo nodded. "My father probably spends more time at White's. But he comes here to catch up with his Scottish connections."

On seeing them approach, the footman rapped the front door. It was opened by a tall, older man in butler's garb who invited them into the vestibule, apologised obsequiously for not recognising them and asked for their names.

"I am Lord Murdo Balfour," Murdo said, "and this is my guest, Mr. Lauriston."

"Forgive me for asking, my lord, but are you a member?"

"I am," Murdo said easily. "Though it is some years since I last visited."

The butler bade them take a seat while he checked the membership records. It didn't take long. The membership ledger showed that Lord Murdo was indeed a member and had been for the last twelve years. Having thus been granted entry, Murdo was also permitted to sign David in as his guest.

"Will you require a table for dinner, my lord?" the butler asked as he ushered them through the vestibule. "We have roast beef this evening, and there's an excellent syllabub."

"Not just now, thank you," Murdo said politely. "I think we will take a look around to begin with."

"Very good, my lord. You will find a number of lounges on this floor. This is where our gentlemen like to meet and converse. The dining rooms are on the next floor, and the card rooms are on the floor above that."

"Thank you," Murdo replied, his cool tone discouraging any further conversation. Taking the hint, the butler nodded and withdrew.

"Come on," Murdo said to David, and they began a tour.

It quickly became plain that, despite the single front door, Culzeans occupied more than one house.

There were four separate lounges of varying sizes on the ground floor, and the rooms had been arranged so that the members could stroll from one to the other with ease. Most of them were crammed with small groupings of comfortable-looking leather armchairs, many of which were occupied by the members and their guests. The fireplaces in each room burned merrily, and candles blazed from sconces on the walls.

It was when they reached the fourth and last lounge that Murdo was hailed by someone he knew.

"Murdoch, my boy! What on earth are you doing here?"

Murdo stopped dead at the sound of his father's cut-glass voice, and David halted slightly behind him. As luck would have it, the marquess hadn't noticed David when he'd first clapped eyes on Murdo, and his tone was warm with mingled surprise and approval, his harsh features lightened by something that looked like real pleasure. A moment later, though—when he saw David at his son's shoulder—the pleasure faded and his mouth tightened into a grim line.

"I see you have your...secretary with you," the marquess added. There was enough of a pause before the word *secretary* to convey his displeasure without alerting his companion, a man with a stiff bearing who looked to be around the same age as the earl, to his true thoughts about David.

Murdo looked up and, after a brief hesitation,

shifted his course to approach his father and the other man.

"Good evening, Father," he said. "Lord Hartley."

Lord Hartley. So this was the man whose daughter Murdo was engaged to.

David had no choice but to follow Murdo. He stayed a little behind him, hovering at his right elbow, noting the cool expression on Lord Hartley's face as he took Murdo's proffered hand and shook it briefly.

"This is my secretary, Mr. Lauriston," Murdo added, standing a little to the side. Hartley gave the slightest of nods, forced to acknowledge David but clearly not pleased to be introduced to so lowly a personage. David bowed politely, though not deeply, in return. The marquess ignored him.

Lord Hartley turned back to Murdo. "I didn't realise you were in town," he murmured, turning to glance at the marquess as though expecting an explanation from him.

"He's only just arrived, haven't you, Murdoch?" the marquess said, smiling tightly.

"Indeed." Murdo gave his father a wintry smile in return, then turned to Hartley. "I was actually planning to call on you tomorrow, my lord. I was hoping we could speak in private. Perhaps in the afternoon?"

The marquess spoke before Hartley had a chance to respond. "I have to attend Parliament tomorrow afternoon. The evening would be better. Perhaps over dinner—"

Murdo interrupted him before he could go further. "You misunderstand, Father," he said mildly. "I wish to speak to Lord Hartley in private."

The earl's lips thinned at that, but Lord Hartley said, "We can talk now, if you wish. There must be a private chamber we can use here."

"I regret I cannot this evening. I am on an errand of some importance."

"More important than speaking with your future father-in-law?" Hartley replied with a slight sharpness to his tone.

Murdo's pause was uncomfortable. "Yes," he said at last. "I'm afraid so."

The earl's expression was pure ice, somehow furious and blank at once.

Hartley plainly wasn't pleased either, but he gave a curt nod. "Very well," he said. "Come to the house at two o'clock tomorrow."

"Thank you." Murdo executed a short, stiff bow. "Please excuse us."

He didn't say anything to David until they were moving through the open doors into the next room.

"Sorry to be so high-handed with you," he murmured, "but you are supposed to be my secretary."

David just gave a soft laugh.

They took the stairs up to the next floor, the dining rooms. These were bustling with patrons partaking of the roast beef, which looked to be rather dry, and the "excellent syllabub", which was, in fact, alarmingly grey. The diners seemed happy enough to wolf their dinners down, though. They weren't here for the food, after all, but for the drink and the cards and, most of all, the company.

David and Murdo looked in each of the three dining rooms but saw no sign of Kinnell. When they came out of the last one, Murdo said, "Let's try the card rooms. It's rather early, but we may as well look."

It was early. The hard gaming that came later and that would have scores of gentlemen crowding round the tables wouldn't begin for a while. Only a small number of older gentlemen were sitting around, enjoying a few hands of cards for what appeared to be modest stakes. And again, there was no sign of Kinnell.

"He must have decided to stay at home this evening, with Elizabeth," David said. The thought made him shiver. What would Kinnell do to her? What about when he discovered she was with child? He pushed that thought away determinedly. Enough time to think about that later when he lay sleepless in bed, as he knew he would tonight.

"Probably," Murdo said. "Let's get back and see whether Liddle's found out any more for us. We have to do something before he gets her out of London."

They made their way back down to the ground

floor, wending their way through the maze of rooms. Murdo wanted to avoid the room he'd seen his father and Hartley in earlier, so he slipped a coin to a footman who took them down a service corridor that bypassed it, leading them straight into the largest and quietest of the lounges, where members could read their newspapers in peace while they drank their port.

At the same moment that David and Murdo entered the lounge, another pair of gentlemen strolled through the door on the opposite side of the room.

One of them was Kinnell.

He was pink-cheeked from the cold, and he was smiling—grinning, in fact—bright-eyed and pleased with himself, seeming well disposed towards his fellow men.

"Bring us your best brandy," he told the same servant who had greeted David and Murdo earlier. "I'm celebrating."

His companion—short, tubby and balding—laughed. "I wish you'd tell me what this celebration is about!"

But Kinnell's glee was already fading. He had seen Murdo, and David, and he was observing their approach. His thin, hawkish features were taut with bristling anger that was kept in check by what David suspected was a touch of fear.

"Yes, do tell, Kinnell," Murdo said with the bland, easy smile he wore when he was masking his thoughts.

"What are you celebrating? Or perhaps I should take a guess?"

Kinnell went to walk past Murdo—to cut him entirely—but Murdo put out a hand, easily detaining him. He *tsk*ed. "Come now, you aren't going to ignore me, are you?" he said. "I do so hate to be ignored!"

Kinnell wasn't a small man, but Murdo topped him by a couple of inches and his broad shoulders dwarfed the other man's thinner frame.

"Let me by," Kinnell gritted out. "We are not friends, but at least let us not make a scene."

Murdo laughed, and his expression was not pleasant. "Ah, but perhaps I want to make a scene," he said, not lowering his voice in the slightest, his big hand still on Kinnell's shoulder. A few heads turned and newspapers were lowered as the encounter began to attract attention.

Once again, Kinnell tried to shrug him off and walk away, but Murdo wouldn't let him. He stepped closer, crowding Kinnell till the other man was forced to take a step back.

"Steady on there!" the tubby man protested weakly.

Murdo turned his head and smiled at him, his geniality oddly unnerving. "Do you want to participate in this conversation? Or are you going to be a good chap and keep your trap shut?"

The tubby man's face burned, and he slunk back, leaving Kinnell alone.

Murdo turned his attention back to Kinnell. "You were looking ever so pleased with yourself when you came in here," he said. "I think you must have been reunited with your lovely young wife. Am I right?"

David caught a flurry of movement at the corner of his eye. He turned his head to see a few more men entering the room. They filed in and leaned against the back wall, blatantly watching the drama. Now it was quiet enough to hear a pin drop.

"Well?" Murdo prompted.

"And what if I have?" Kinnell bit out, a faint sneer of triumph lifting his thin upper lip.

"No, it can't just be that," Murdo mused, tapping his chin with his forefinger. "You look far too happy for merely that. Oh, wait, I have it! Did you give her a sound thrashing before you came out? Now *that'd* put a smile on your face, wouldn't it? You do enjoy handing out a thrashing. Especially to someone smaller and weaker than you."

There were a few gasps at that, and Kinnell went white.

"How dare you!" he hissed.

Murdo's gaze bored into him. "Tell me I'm wrong," he said. "I'd love to be wrong, believe me. But I fear Elizabeth is probably tending her injuries as we speak."

"Do not call *my wife* by her given name!" Kinnell shouted, pushing Murdo's arm away. He managed it this time, but his voice shook with what sounded like real fear when Murdo stepped into his path to stop him passing, making him halt in his tracks.

"Enough of this, Balfour," a deep voice interjected from the back of the room. "She's his wife and his business. Leave it be."

Balfour didn't even look round. "Stay out of this. Anyone who cares to stand at the shoulder of this *dog* is going to get the same that's coming to him."

Whoever it was that had spoken fell silent. Murdo smiled at Kinnell. A wolf considering how to take down its prey.

Kinnell tried to gather his dignity about him, but his fear was pouring off him now. He cast a look of loathing at David.

"Is this what comes of *associating* with commoners?" Kinnell loaded his words with enough disgust to clearly imply that there was something untoward about David. David kept his eyes on Murdo and Kinnell, but he felt the gazes of the audience to this drama moving over him. Heard their murmurings as they speculated about his identity.

Fortified by the reaction of the onlookers, Kinnell added more arrogantly, "Besides, what business of yours is my wife?"

Murdo smiled again, and again David thought of a wolf, that unblinking regard, that predatory stillness. Kinnell's arrogance faltered. He saw that Murdo was pleased by the question and couldn't understand why.

"Oh, your wife is very much my business," he said, his voice ringing clearly for all to hear. "When she left you, she came to me. She's been sharing my bed for months."

"No, Murdo—" David said, horrified, but no one paid him any attention. Every gaze was fixed on Murdo and Kinnell.

Murdo was moving in for the kill now, stepping right up to Kinnell, crowding him till the man had to step back to put space between them. Step back and then step back again, till he collided with a table and could go no farther.

"Murdoch—for God's sake!"

David turned—everyone did, every head in the room swinging round to see the Marquess of Balfour standing in the doorway on the other side of the room, Hartley at his elbow. The earl's expression was rigid with shock and fury, and Hartley looked ready to have an apoplexy, his already ruddy features practically puce.

"It's not true," Kinnell said loudly, and, of course, it wasn't. But no one would ever believe that. Murdo had just delivered a staggering insult, and everyone present realised there was only one way a gentleman of honour could react to such an insult. A cold blade of panic slid into David's gut as he waited for the inevitable.

"What kind of man are you?" Murdo taunted. "If you had any self-respect, you would throw your glove in my face right now. But you're too much of a coward."

There were gasps at that, and a few shouted protests from their audience. Bad enough to call the man out for cruelty and announce you were his wife's lover. But to call him a coward? The men gathered around waited, impatient for Kinnell to do the right thing.

Kinnell looked sick with misery and fear, but he knew too. There was no escape from this, not with any pride or honour left intact. At last, he lifted his arm and dragged his glove off with shaking fingers. The blow he struck to Murdo's cheek had little vigour, and Murdo merely grinned to feel its impact.

"I demand satisfaction," Kinnell said, his gaze bleak. "Name your second."

Murdo's wolf smile grew. "Mr. Lauriston will be my second. And yours?"

Kinnell looked about the room. The companion he'd arrived with appeared to have melted away entirely. He scanned the crowd of observers.

"Lennox?" he said at last. "Would you?"

The onlookers parted, and a man stepped forward, a man David knew very well. David's heart began to thud in his chest as the man's gaze flickered briefly to David, then back to Kinnell. His face—that once dear, familiar face—carried a trace of panic, but when he answered Kinnell, his voice was sure.

"I will," said Sir William Lennox.

Will Lennox. David's first love. The man who had once broken his heart.

Once the challenge had been issued and accepted, a number of the gentlemen stepped forward to offer their advice. The two principals were separated, and an older gentleman, a military type, took it upon himself to educate the two seconds on their duties and obligations, ushering them over to a group of chairs on the far side of the room.

"Do you know each other?" he asked first.

David opened his mouth, but before he could speak, Will held out a hand.

"Sir William Lennox," he said. "And you are?"

David followed his lead, disappointed and relieved at once. "David Lauriston."

They shook hands briefly. A distant part of David's mind noted that Will had lost the willowy grace of his youth and the prettiness of his boyhood features. His features had settled into a blander maturity, though he was a pleasant-looking man.

Their guide introduced himself as Major Donaldson. They sat down to listen while he explained the business of how a duel worked. In the first instance, he began, the seconds should meet, to see what could be done to resolve matters by apology or otherwise. If that wasn't possible, there were arrangements to be made—a location to be agreed upon, weapons to be approved, a surgeon's services to be secured. The major sent a footman for pen and ink so he could write down the name and direction of a surgeon who was discreet and "good at patching up bullet wounds".

David listened attentively, even as his heart beat hard with panic and his stomach churned at the thought of Murdo coming to harm. Strange, he thought as he watched the major laboriously scribe his recommendation, that when he finally came face-to-face with Will Lennox, he could think of nothing but Murdo. He had spent years thinking about what he would say to Will if they ever met again. How he would tear up at Will over the other man's long-ago betrayal—telling David's father that the kiss the older man had witnessed between them had all been David's doing, and leaving him to face the consequences alone.

And now he realised that he had nothing he wanted to say to Will at all.

Will was writing now—his address for David's visit the next morning. When he was finished, he handed the paper to David, and all three men stood up.

"I'll leave you gentlemen to your arrangements, then," the major said, giving a stiff little bow.

David and Will murmured their gratitude and their farewells.

When the major had gone, Will turned back to David. "Will ten o'clock tomorrow morning suit?" he asked, all politeness.

"That will be fine," David said, tucking Will's address into his pocket. "Now, if you'll excuse me, I should find Lord Murdo." He went to move away but Will detained him with a hand on his forearm.

"Davy, listen—"

Their eyes met, and for a moment, David was taken back years. That moss-green gaze was still so very familiar. Then he shook himself and pulled his arm free.

"Don't call me that," he said and walked away.

Murdo had been taken to another room. He sat in an armchair beside the fireplace, staring at the flames. Several other men milled around, murmuring, but none of them spoke to Murdo.

He didn't look up when David entered the room. It was only when David stood directly in front of him, on the hearth rug, that he finally tore his gaze away from the fire.

"You're back," he said, his expression oddly guarded.

"Yes," David replied stiffly, conscious of their audience. "I've arranged to meet Sir William tomorrow morning. Shall we go—" He was about to add *home* but stopped himself at the last moment, making his words sound oddly cut off and awkward.

Murdo nodded and rose from his chair. They weren't quite halfway across the room when Hartley appeared in the doorway, the marquess slightly behind him. It seemed the night's confrontations were not yet over.

Murdo stepped slightly in front of David in a subtly protective gesture.

Hartley didn't waste any time on bluster. "Lord Murdo, you may take it that your engagement to my daughter is at an end as of this moment," he announced loudly. His face was cold and expressionless, and somehow his words sounded all the more powerful for the lack of emotion in them.

The audience for this encounter was smaller than for the one with Kinnell, but this was no less public. This evening's events would be the talk of every drawing room in London come tomorrow afternoon.

"Neither I nor any of my family will acknowledge you after this moment," Hartley continued. He paused before adding, "You have brought shame on your father's name. If you were my son, I would disown you." He turned to the earl. "You have my pity, Balfour," he added, then stalked out of the room, leaving Murdo to face his father.

Another glove thrown down, David thought. By Hartley this time, for the earl. And David somehow knew it was a glove the marquess would not want to pick up.

"If you were my son, I would disown you."

Hartley was a man of considerable political power, a Tory, like Balfour. The marriage of their children could have been the start of a new political dynasty.

For three decades, the marquess had determinedly set about binding Murdo to him. His ropes were made of secrets and threats and promises, and he had stubbornly held on to every one, resisting his son's attempts to get free of him.

All of his efforts had been leading up to this marriage. And now it would not happen.

The knot of ropes that bound Murdo to his father was Gordian in its complexity and subtlety. Tonight, Murdo had swept a sword through it, disdaining its cleverness. Severing it with determination and without concern for the consequences.

David watched the earl. Examining that cold, harsh face for clues to his anger and frustration, wary of his ire. He was ready to see evidence of every one of those emotions. What he was not prepared for was what he actually saw.

Naked grief.

The small audience of men in the room waited for the marquess to speak, and Murdo waited too, seeming resigned. Even so, the earl's decision did not come easily. He did not want to do what needed to be done. But when all was said and done, he was a politician and a pillar of respectability. And he had been put in a position that offered him no alternative.

At last, his voice ringing out over the silence, he said, "You are no son of mine."

Then he turned and walked away, his shoulders rounded with defeat.

Chapter Sixteen

Shortly after the Marquess left, the servant who had first greeted David and Murdo earlier that evening approached them. He carried their greatcoats and hats in his arms.

"My lord," he said, bowing to Murdo, then turning to David, "Sir." He paused, a patient, pleasant expression on his long, thin face.

David glanced at Murdo, who looked coolly amused.

"I believe," he informed David, "we are being asked to leave."

The servant managed to demur politely, even as he handed them their hats and held their greatcoats open while they shrugged into them. The group of men who had watched the confrontation between Murdo and his father continued to silently observe, with grim, disapproving faces, as Murdo and David readied themselves to leave.

David wondered whether, despite Murdo's unfazed demeanour, the judgment and disapproval of these men weighed on him. Surely it must do—it weighed on David and these men were nothing to him. To Murdo, they were his peers, men he'd been educated with, socialised and done business with. He didn't have to like or respect them to feel injured by their treatment of him.

As they walked from the smaller lounge into the larger one, it was worse. Every head turned, and the murmurings of conversations came to an abrupt halt. But Murdo didn't even seem to notice. He had spied Kinnell on the other side of the room.

Kinnell was ready to leave too, his companion from earlier back at his side. His eyes widened in alarm to see Murdo, and he turned away, making for the door.

"I hear a swift bullet to the brain is more merciful than one to the guts, Kinnell," Murdo called after him. "If you don't want your death to be slow and painful, do not lay a hand on your wife tonight."

Angry murmurings rose at that further insult, and David took hold of Murdo's upper arm, afraid he would go after Kinnell again and stir the ire of the men present. There was no doubt that Murdo was the villain of this piece in their minds, despite the accusations Murdo had levelled about Kinnell's brutality.

Kinnell didn't look round at Murdo's threat, but he'd heard, all right. David was glad to see the hesitation in his step before he moved on. Perhaps he'd think twice before raising his hand to Elizabeth again tonight.

As Kinnell disappeared, a slight, nondescript man approached them. He looked like a clerk, anonymous and somewhat out of place amongst the elegant aristocrats surrounding him.

"Lord Murdo," the man said, stopping in front of them. "I wonder if I might have a private word with you and your friend? I am the owner of this establishment, Mr. Robertson."

Murdo glanced at the man and became, in an instant, the archetypal aristocrat, expressing with a single raised brow cool astonishment at being so addressed. To his credit, Robertson didn't flinch, and at length Murdo shrugged.

"Very well."

"This way, please."

Murdo followed Robertson out of the room, and David trailed behind them, horribly conscious of the silent scrutiny of the crowd.

Robertson led them into the vestibule where they'd waited when they first arrived, closing the door with exaggerated care. He turned round, a composed fellow in his clerkish way.

"I am afraid I must apologise, Lord Murdo," he began. "I understand that earlier this evening my employee, Mr. Hill, informed you that your membership of this club remained valid."

David's stomach churned as he realised what was

coming.

"He did," Murdo said.

Robertson shrugged, all embarrassed apology. He was good at this.

"Mr. Hill was mistaken. It has been so long since you visited that your membership has...lapsed."

"Ah, lapsed, is it?" Amusement teased at one corner of Murdo's generous mouth. He seemed perfectly unconcerned by this development, though David knew how good he was at concealing his true feelings.

"I'm afraid so, my lord. You are welcome, of course, to apply for membership again..." He trailed off, his carefully schooled expression implying, without words, that such an effort would be a waste of time.

"Tempting as that is," Murdo replied dryly, "there would be little point. I am moving my household permanently to Scotland in the near future."

Robertson was too good to let his relief show.

"Of course, my lord. I understand." And with that, the little man gave a deep bow and stepped back.

An instant later, the front door that led onto the street opened, held in place by the same impassive footman who'd stood entry when they first arrived.

And Murdo left Culzeans, never to return.

Murdo was quiet on the way back to Curzon Street, and David was too. The events of the last hour weighed heavily upon them both. David had believed they were going to Culzeans to talk to Kinnell, perhaps to begin a negotiation. He hadn't expected an irrevocable confrontation. Now he sat in the carriage, sharp anxiety for Murdo churning in his gut, his too-vivid imagination conjuring images of Murdo with a bullet hole in his head, falling to the ground, again and again.

"Why did you do it?" David said at last, puncturing the silence. "What were you thinking?"

Murdo turned his head. He was strangely calm, though his jaw had an obstinate thrust to it.

"It wasn't planned," he said. "Not that it hadn't occurred to me—it had—but not as something I would actually do."

"What did you plan, then?"

Murdo shrugged. "A more subtle threat. Kinnell's estate, Marloch, is burdened by sizeable debts. I thought I'd let it be known I was minded to acquire some of them and take Marloch for myself."

"Then why the change?"

"Two reasons. It would take months to implement that sort of plan. Once I laid eyes on Kinnell tonight and thought about what he'd likely done to his wife today, I wanted to do something to stop him now."

David could understand that. He'd wanted to lay into the bastard with his bare fists and show him what it felt like to be beaten. "What was the other reason?"

"Seeing my father and Hartley. I felt the noose tightening, and I realised that I needed to do something drastic if I were to free myself."

"You've put your life in danger just to free yourself from your engagement?" David exclaimed.

"I count it a good result," Murdo said, with a distinct edge to his voice. "My engagement has been brought to an end and in a way that paints me as the villain and the lady as entirely blameless. What more could you want, David? Surely that's enough, even for you?"

"That you live to see it?" David hated that his voice trembled with emotion. He felt rather than saw the glance that Murdo shot him, his big body suddenly very still and watchful.

"I'll live to see it," Murdo said after a pause. "Kinnell won't go through with the duel."

"You can't be certain of that."

Another shrug. "Even if he does go through with it, I'll win, and he knows it. I'm an excellent shot—I'm well known for it. It's one of the reasons everyone was so aggrieved on his behalf tonight. They thought it unsportsmanlike of me to put a man with so little ability in the position of having to challenge me."

"And if you win, you'll be a murderer," David said bitterly, though in truth, he did feel better to at least know that everyone expected Murdo to prevail.

"If that happens, I'll flee to the continent," Murdo said. He leaned closer, putting one long, gloved finger beneath David's chin and tipping it up, forcing David to meet his ink-black gaze. Murdo smiled crookedly, though there was still a hard look about his eyes that puzzled David. "And if my lover—my *male* lover—accompanies me, it'll be the biggest scandal in twenty years."

Even if that was nonsense talk, it made David's heart beat a little faster. A wave of mingled excitement and anxiety washed over his heart, and on impulse he reached for Murdo, pulling him close enough to bring their mouths together in a desperate kiss, needing to feel Murdo warm and alive against him.

For an instant, Murdo hesitated, as though surprised, then he sighed against David's mouth and wound his brawny arms tightly round David's leaner body, deepening the kiss.

When he finally pulled back, breathing hard, it was to say something that David wasn't expecting.

"So—when were you going to mention that Sir William Lennox is your Will?"

David stared at him in astonishment. It was dark in the carriage, but he'd had time to get used to it, and he could make out the glitter in Murdo's eyes and the faintly belligerent set of his jaw. Was this the cause of the suppressed anger David had detected since they'd left Culzeans?

"You know about him?"

"I've known for ages. You told me months ago about Will, the boy who broke your heart, the boy from the big house in Midlauder. It didn't take much effort to discover who owned the big house in Midlauder."

"You were checking up on me?"

"I wondered about my competition, yes."

"Competition?" David repeated. "How could Will possibly be competition? He broke with me years ago. Tonight's the first time I've seen him in nearly ten years."

"I saw the way he looked at you," Murdo retorted, suddenly intense.

"What? Are you mad?"

Murdo laughed, though he sounded far from amused. "No, but you're blind. I'll wager he'll try to get you into his bed when you see him tomorrow."

David just stared at him. It was ridiculous. So far from any remote possibility that it would've been funny were it not for the fact that Murdo seemed to be deadly serious.

"I can assure you that won't happen. Will has no interest in me." Even as he said it, an insidious memory intruded—of Will's hand on his forearm and the murmur of David's old name on the other man's lips.

"Davy—"

But that really was ridiculous. He shook his head to dislodge the thought.

Murdo stayed silent, his mouth set in a mutinous line, unconvinced. A bolt of tenderness struck at David to see Murdo's obvious unhappiness, and his next words were gentle.

"Murdo, Will's not like us. He chose to marry, chose to be with a *woman*—" When Murdo gave a harsh laugh, David broke off. "What?"

"You. You're so naïve." Murdo smiled thinly, leaning closer. "Over the years, I've seen your Will at a number of, well, let's call them evening entertainments, and I can tell you that he's as much like you and I as it's possible to be. I've seen him with my own eyes. He likes to be watched, you know. The last time, as I recall, he had his cock buried in a grenadier guard and—"

"Jesus, Murdo, stop!"

David recoiled, sickened. Horror swamped him— that Murdo had known all about Will, and about his indiscretions, and never said. That he had hugged the knowledge to himself and let David demonstrate his foolish naïveté before he said even one word.

Murdo leaned in even closer.

"Why should I stop?" he hissed, his mouth twisted in a savage snarl. "Prefer the fantasy, do you? The pure boy who wouldn't let you so much as touch him? The love of your fucking life?"

"He's not the love of my life, you idiot!" David snapped, incensed by Murdo's obtuseness. "You are!"

For a long moment, neither of them said anything. David's breath was coming hard with unfamiliar anger, and Murdo was staring at him, eyes wide with almost comical astonishment.

"Did you—" Murdo began. "That is... What did you say?"

David glanced away, heart thudding now. "You heard me."

There was another long pause, then Murdo said, "You know, you really shouldn't say something like that if you don't mean it." His voice shook slightly.

David looked up at that, to encounter an expression he rarely saw on Murdo's face: uncertainty.

"Of course I mean it," he replied. "Have you ever known me to say something I don't mean?"

Murdo thought about that. "No. No, I haven't." He closed his eyes, then swallowed. "It's just, I've loved you for so long, David. I really didn't think you felt the same way."

"Wh-what?" David stuttered. "How could you think that? And wait... You love me?"

"Yes, of course. Isn't it obvious?"

"No! Though how you can say that you didn't think *I* loved *you*—" He broke off, his voice cracking with disbelief.

"You've never seemed to want what I want. You're always telling me that what we have can't last, that we have to be careful. Always reminding me that you'll be leaving me soon." Murdo swallowed. "To be frank, I feared that if I told you how I felt, it would only make you leave all the sooner."

Even in the shadowy carriage, David could see the private grief written in Murdo's dark, liquid gaze. It made David's heart hurt. He raised his hand to touch Murdo's face, tracing the strong, determined line of the other man's jaw, running the pad of his thumb over those wide, generous lips. This man, whose face was now as familiar to David as his own, had harboured these secrets from him, and he hated that. Hated especially that everything Murdo had just mentioned—David's constant reminders that they could not stay together, that he had to leave—came from David putting the world first and Murdo second.

"Love should not be denied."

"God, I'm sorry," he whispered, appalled. "I'm so very sorry. You deserve more."

David felt like he was breaking open, like the truth was tearing its way out of him. Somehow, Murdo had become more important to him than anything else. Everything he'd worked for—respectability, a shining career, wealth—all of it would be ashes in his mouth if he lost Murdo.

"To hell with what I deserve," Murdo whispered. "All I want is you."

Chapter Seventeen

When they got back to Curzon Street, Liddle opened the door. David wondered if the man ever rested.

"My lord, your father arrived a short while ago. He is waiting for you in the drawing room."

Murdo absorbed that news. "And Mr. MacLennan?"

"In his bedchamber, sir. I made sure the marquess did not see him."

Murdo nodded. "Good man." He turned to look at David. "Would you come with me?"

"To see your father?" David asked uncertainly.

"If you wouldn't mind."

"All right, if you're sure that's wise." David's uncertain tone betrayed his scepticism.

Murdo managed a weak smile. "I'm not sure at all, but I'd like you to be there."

David followed Murdo down the candlelit corridor and into the drawing room where the marquess was waiting. The older man sat in the same winged armchair he'd selected the last time he'd come. It was the obviously dominant chair in the room, the master's chair. A goblet of some spirit—brandy perhaps, or whisky—rested on the occasional table beside him, untouched.

He looked up, his eyes going first to Murdo and then to David.

"Send your catamite away," he said. "I wish to speak to you alone."

"If you want to speak to me at all, you will do so in Mr. Lauriston's presence." Murdo turned to David and smiled. "Please excuse my father's manners, Mr. Lauriston, and do take a seat."

"*Mister* Lauriston, is it?" the marquess mocked as David lowered himself onto a straight-backed chair, glad to rest his leg. "A nice title for a whore."

Murdo's expression didn't alter, but he said coolly, "You know he's not a whore. You know exactly who and what he is, don't you?"

The marquess laughed, an ugly sound. "Of course. He's a lawyer, but his family are peasant stock. As low as they come."

Did the man think such words would insult him, David wondered? He felt no shame over his origins. Quite the contrary, in fact. He stared at the earl, saying nothing, waiting for Murdo to reply.

Murdo didn't seem inclined to speak either. He simply stood, watching his father until, eventually, the marquess was forced to break the silence.

"You are a fool, Murdoch," he said. His words dripped with bitterness and with something else—bewilderment.

Murdo smiled and shrugged. "Maybe so. Is that all you came to tell me, or is there more to come? If so, I'll help myself to a drink before we go further."

Without waiting for an answer, he went to the sideboard where a decanter and glasses sat. Removing the crystal stopper, he poured two generous measures into a pair of goblets.

"Just tell me this: why did you do it?" the marquess bit out.

Murdo crossed the floor, halting in front of David to offer one of the goblets to him. David took it, his fingers brushing Murdo's as they transferred the glass between them. He found the tiny touch oddly comforting and hoped it was comforting to Murdo too.

Murdo didn't take a seat. Instead, he stood at the fireplace, resting his elbow on the mantel. He was able to look down at his father from there, giving himself the advantage of height, since his father had commandeered the master's chair in his son's own house.

"You wouldn't understand," Murdo said. "It was…a rescue mission."

The marquess shook his head in disbelief. "To what end? So, Sir Alasdair Kinnell thrashes his wife every now and again? She made her bed when she married him, and it's not as though you're bedding her. Whatever you said tonight, I know *that's* not the case!"

David found himself on his feet without having made the conscious decision to stand. A jolt of pain travelled down his leg from hip to knee, but he managed to suppress a gasp.

"You will not speak of that lady again," he said in a deadly voice. "You are not fit to lick her boots."

The marquess smiled, eyeing David's reaction with undisguised interest.

"Do not react to my father's jibes," Murdo said to David. "He'll only do it more. He enjoys riling people."

The marquess laughed then, a soft, appreciative sound. "You know me so well, Murdoch," he said. There was a pause—a few heartbeats—and then his faintly amused expression faded into something undeniably sorrowful.

"You were the only one, out of the three of you. The only one I had real hopes of."

"What rot," Murdoch said mildly. "There are no two sons more obedient than Harris and Iain. I am the only who ever defied you."

"And you are the only one with wit, with ability. You are the only one who sees the world as it is. Oh, Harris will get the title and the lands. What of it? You could have had so much more than that. You could have been a kingmaker, Murdoch. You could have risen to the highest reaches of power. *That* is what I wanted for you! That is what this marriage was about—and you *know* that! When I brokered it for you, you were in agreement—"

"You mean, I did not protest," Murdo put in.

"Do not play the puppet with me. You intended to come back to London and follow the path we'd always talked about."

"Become like you," Murdo said, expressionless. "Rise through the ranks, the real influence behind the public face of government."

"Yes, and you could've done it. But, instead, you went running off to Scotland—to *him*"—he gestured at David—"and ignored all the summonses I sent you. Why?"

"I came to my senses."

"Came to your senses? You will never be received in polite society again! You think any of those men who like to invest in those schemes that make you so much money will send you a brass farthing once they hear of this scandal? You will be a *pariah*, Murdoch."

Murdo shrugged. "True, but there is nothing to be done about it now." He paused. "It's amusing, actually. For all these years, you've held the possibility of ruin over my head, and here I go and do it by myself. All that power you had over me, and until tonight, I never realised how flimsy it really was. All I needed to do was renounce everything you ever gave me. Which wasn't so very difficult once I realised how little I wanted it."

"You'll be well satisfied, then, now that you have nothing," the marquess snapped.

"That's not how I see it."

The marquess glanced at David, understanding dawning. "I see," he said, adding after a moment, "Well, I wish you'd told me rather than falling on your sword like this. I'm sure we could have come to some sort of accommodation. There aren't many beds of married love in this city. It's not so difficult to arrange a house, privacy—"

Murdo laughed with what sounded like genuine amusement this time. "You don't expect me to believe you'd have come to an *accommodation* with me? You, who always said a man keeps secrets at his peril."

The earl's lips thinned. "If you had told me—"

Murdo didn't let him go further. "If I'd told you, you would have done everything you could to sabotage it," he snapped. "And anyone who stood in your way would have been destroyed."

The marquess fell silent. He didn't protest or indeed say anything.

Murdo turned to David. "Here's a story for you: when I was boy, I lived for the summers. We spent them at Kilbeigh, in Argyllshire—my mother and my siblings and me. Not my father. He was always too busy in London." He turned to his father. "It must be years since you were in Scotland."

The marquess said nothing, and Murdo turned back to David. "When I was sixteen, I told my father I wanted to stay at Kilbeigh. Manage the estate for my brother Harris, who was to inherit the title. That way Harris could stay in London and take his seat in the Lords. I thought that would satisfy my father's desire for one of his sons to follow in his political footsteps. I knew Harris would be perfectly happy, so long as his allowance was being paid."

"Harris isn't like you. He hasn't the wit for politics," the marquess interrupted, but Murdo ignored him.

"My father surprised me," he told David. "He was encouraging. He said that he would arrange for me spend some time with Mr. Mure, the senior land agent at Kilbeigh, to see if I liked the work. I was sent to Kilbeigh on my own, in the family carriage. I felt like a man for the first time in my life."

David wanted to tell him to stop. He knew something was coming that was awful, and part of him didn't want to hear it—except that he knew Murdo needed to say it, and he needed David to be his witness.

Murdo smiled at him, and his gaze was unbearably sad. "One day, after I'd been home a few days, Mr. Mure told me we were going out early. I was to be saddled and ready for seven o'clock the next day. I remember getting dressed that morning, wondering what the day would bring. As soon as I got down to the stables, I knew—" He broke off.

"What?" David said, prompting him. "What did you know?"

"I knew that something was wrong," Murdo continued, swallowing. "There were redcoats in the stable yard, and a clerk from the sheriff's office. He had legal papers. Once we were on our way, I asked Mr. Mure what was going on, and he told me that it was an eviction. I didn't know what to expect. Certainly not the burning down of an entire village."

Oh God, no.

David's heart wrenched as he remembered another conversation, in another drawing room, months ago. David had spoken of the clearance of the highlanders from their ancestral lands. Had accused Murdo of exactly this.

"You're a highlander, aren't you? The son of the laird himself. Did your father evict any of his tenants from their homelands to make room for sheep? Burn down any houses?"

Murdo had begged him to stop.

"I'm so sorry—" David whispered now.

"That day cured me of any wish to manage Kilbeigh," Murdo said now. "As my father knew it would. But then, you've always been such a student of human nature, haven't you, Father?" He turned back to the marquess now, who sat in the winged armchair, looking remote and defiant. "You always know just the thing to do, to persuade, to cajole…"

"It would have been such a waste," the marquess said, his voice clipped. "You had so much potential, even then."

"I loved Kilbeigh," Murdo said. "I was happy there."

The marquess shrugged. "Happiness comes and goes," he said. "The ability to shape the future direction of this kingdom, though—that is something that few men can boast a part in. That is what I offered you."

"And I have thrown it away."

"Yes, you have." The marquess rubbed his hands over his face in a gesture of supreme weariness. "You have thrown it away," he repeated, and this time it sounded like he was coming to understand that it could not be undone.

"This evening, you publicly disowned me," Murdo said. "That is not something you will go back on."

"No, it is not," the marquess admitted. "All the way over here, I tried to think of a way out of this, but there is none. There is nothing I can do to save you from your own foolishness. There were so many witnesses. It will be an immense scandal. I have to disassociate the rest of the family from you entirely."

"I understand," Murdo said. "I will not embarrass

you by showing my face around Town. I'm going back to Scotland after this, and I don't intend to come back."

"Good," the marquess replied, but his face belied the word on his lips. He looked devastated. And David realised, in that moment, that in his own way, the marquess loved his son.

Murdo took a deep breath. "I don't ask much in return. Only—"

"Only?" A brief glimmer, of hope perhaps, lit the earl's gaze. That if Murdo wanted something of him, after all...

"Only—that you leave us alone."

Us.

The glimmer of hope in the earl's gaze faded and died.

"Murdoch," he said, and there was a wealth of pain and regret in the word. "You achieved something tonight I'd never have thought you capable of. You rendered yourself entirely useless to me. I can't do anything with you."

"I know."

The marquess closed his eyes for a long moment. When he opened them again, he said, "Do you remember confronting me about the eviction, all those years ago?"

Murdo nodded, slowly.

"You said you were going to get back at me one

day. And I said that was foolish, that revenge only for revenge's sake served no purpose. It is a waste of energy you could use more productively elsewhere."

"I remember it well," Murdo said. "You said that revenge is only meaningful if it furthers some other objective. Otherwise it is merely the bite of a dog. You said that any fool can wield a whip; the trick is in bringing the horse over the line."

"Quite so," the marquess said and smiled faintly, a ghost of remembered pride. He rose from his chair and crossed the room to stand an arm's length from his son.

"You have put yourself out of the race, Murdoch," he said. "I don't flog dead horses. In fact, I don't grant them another moment of my attention."

For a long moment, the two men gazed at one another.

"Thank you," Murdo said.

The earl's expression grew hard then, and bitter. "Don't thank me," he bit out. "One day you're going to look at your life, and you're going to realise he wasn't worth all this sacrifice."

Murdo didn't say anything, just gazed steadily at his father, waiting.

The marquess shook his head and turned away. "You are the greatest disappointment of my life," he said.

Then he walked out of the room without another word.

Chapter Eighteen

The next morning dawned blustery and cold. Grey clouds scudded around the sky as David made his way to the Lennox residence and the wind buffeted him, forcing him to grab hold of his hat several times. March was coming in like a lion this year.

Will's house was smaller and less grand than Murdo's, a red-brick affair in a less salubrious, though still respectable, corner of London. David's stomach gripped with nerves as he knocked at the door, wondering what reception he could expect.

"Sir William said you were to be brought straight to the study, sir," the grim-faced butler told him. "If you'd care to follow me."

He escorted David down a narrow hallway, stopping in front of one of the doors to lightly knock.

"Enter," came the voice from within.

It was just one word, but unmistakably, it was Will. An aristocratic inflection to it, like Murdo's, but Will's accent was more obviously Scottish. The voice of a country gentleman who'd played with the local children when he was a boy and been tutored at home.

The butler opened the door, inviting David to precede him into the room with a sweeping gesture, and David crossed the threshold into a cosy study. Will had evidently been sitting behind his desk. He was already in the act of rising when David entered. They moved towards one another, coming to a mutual halt in the middle of a Turkish rug in front of the fireplace.

"Mr. Lauriston," he said with a careful smile.

"Sir William." David shook the offered hand as quickly as was decent before drawing his fingers free. Behind him, the click of the door signalled Will's servant had withdrawn, and they were alone.

There was a long pause, then Will said, "I see you have a cane now?"

"It's temporary," David replied shortly.

"What happened?"

"Nothing much. An accident. I am all but recovered." David forced himself to look at the other man, keeping his own expression determinedly blank.

"You certainly look well," Will said at last, and his gaze travelled over David, up, then down. Not too obviously, but obvious enough, to men like them. Had he looked at his grenadier guard like that, David wondered, before he fucked him in front of an audience?

"So do you," David said blandly, giving no hint of his thoughts. He added coolly, "Marriage must agree with you."

Will didn't respond to that, but his gaze, so very direct a moment ago, slid away.

"I hear you have a daughter," David added, all polite interest.

"And a son now," Will confirmed.

"My felicitations."

Will nodded dismissively, apparently disinclined to discuss his children with David. "Would you like a nip of something?" he asked, gesturing at a decanter of something amber on his desk.

At ten o'clock in the morning?

"No, thank you," David murmured. "But I wouldn't mind sitting down."

"Oh, of course," Will replied, glancing at the cane in David's hand. "I should have offered before."

He should have, David thought. But then, Will had never been the most thoughtful of men.

It was an idle observation, but one that pulled him up oddly short. He'd cursed Will Lennox plenty of times over the last decade, but never for anything less dramatic than breaking David's heart. The sheer banality of this reaction—disapproving of the man's manners, for God's sake—struck him as somewhat anticlimactic.

David busied himself, selecting a chair and easing himself carefully into it. The last few days and nights had taken a toll upon him, and he found himself leaning on his cane more than usual.

When he looked up, he caught Will watching him, a fact that made him feel uncomfortable and oddly resentful.

"So," he said evenly, "I've never been involved in a matter like this before, but I understand we're supposed to ascertain if the disagreement between our principals is capable of resolution before we make the arrangements, are we not?"

Will gazed at him for a long moment, then he said, "It's an unhappy situation. Lord Murdo forced Sir Alasdair to make that challenge, and everyone knows it. If the duel proceeds and Sir Alasdair is killed, it will be nothing short of murder. The only honourable way out is for Balfour to offer an apology."

"As to that, Lord Murdo is only prepared to offer an apology on certain conditions," David replied smoothly. "In return, however, Kinnell will get his apology and his honour will be satisfied without any risk to his person. Since Lord Murdo is intent upon withdrawing from society after this incident, Kinnell will not be brought face-to-face with any reminder of it again."

"What sort of conditions?"

"I'm not at liberty to say. Lord Murdo is only prepared to discuss them with Kinnell. I am merely instructed to convey to you that if Kinnell is willing to explore matters further, Lord Murdo will call upon him today at two o'clock this afternoon." David paused. "If not, I will return this evening to discuss arrangements for them to meet."

Will raised an eyebrow, though, to his credit, he did not probe for more information. "Very well," he said. "I'll pass the message on and send a note to let you know his answer."

They stared at one another for a long, uncomfortable moment. As quick as that their business was over—it hadn't been worth the effort of sitting down after all.

"I'll take my leave, then, and await hearing from you further," David said. "I'm staying with Lord Murdo at his house on Curzon Street, if you could send word there." He braced his hands on his thighs and levered himself up, suppressing a wince and reaching for his cane.

Will rose too. "I must say, I find it very curious," he said.

"What?"

"Lord Murdo's announcement regarding Kinnell's wife. I didn't think—well, to be frank, I didn't think he favoured women."

David met Will's familiar green gaze but said nothing.

"And you're staying with him…" Will added, letting his words trail off meaningfully.

Although he'd expected this, David found he still balked at the other man's intrusiveness.

"After my accident, I accepted a position at Lord Murdo's estate in Perthshire to deal with some legal matters for him," David said mildly. "It suited me while I was recuperating."

"Come on, Davy," Will said, drawing closer. His eyes danced with amusement and barely concealed sexual interest. "It can't be a coincidence. I *know* you, remember?" He stretched out his hand and touched David's forearm, stroking his palm upwards. "I know what you are. And if you've spent any time with Murdo Balfour, you won't be the same shy boy I once knew."

David felt sick, watching him, seeing the flirtatious look in his gaze and the promise in that stroking hand.

"You've certainly changed," David got out from behind numb lips. "You used to be quite shy yourself."

"Ah, well, that was back when I was petrified of my own shadow. I've changed since then. Marriage can be curiously liberating."

"Does your wife think so?"

Will's lips tightened, but he shrugged, feigning unconcern. "Her opinion hardly matters."

And wasn't that telling? Perhaps it was no wonder he and Kinnell were friends.

David stepped back, and Will's arm fell down, useless between them.

"I have to go," David said. "I have other matters to attend to today." That was a lie, but David didn't care.

Suddenly, he couldn't wait to leave.

"That's a shame," Will replied warmly, seeming undeterred by David's blatant lack of interest. "Once this duel is dealt with, perhaps we could meet up? Not here, of course, but there's a hotel I know that's discreet and reliable…"

David felt ill at the thought. "I don't think so."

Will's face flushed at David's rejection. "Is this because of what happened before?" he said, "With your father? For God's sake, Davy, we were sixteen. What did you expect?"

I expected you not to lie about your own part in that kiss.

I expected you not to leave me to face the consequences of what happened alone.

Once upon a time, he'd wanted to say that to Will, and more besides. He'd wanted to demand answers. And maybe, stupidly, he'd hoped for an explanation that he could become reconciled to, that could allow him to love Will again.

Not now.

Now he just wanted to forget he'd ever known him. And refusing to answer his question felt like a little bit of revenge for all those pleading letters he'd sent years before, none of which had ever prompted a single response.

"As I said," David repeated, "I really must go."

"It won't last, you know," Will said. "Murdo Balfour might fancy you now, but his interest will fade. He's had more men than I've had hot suppers, and one day he'll get married, just like me. Our sort always do."

For a moment, David stared at him, at this long-lost love of his.

He was a stranger. A blandly handsome man of means, surrounded by his Turkish rugs and leather-bound books. A man with riches and a well-bred wife and two children already in the nursery.

Perhaps he had everything he wanted.

David thought of the old Will, then—of the beautiful boy whose green eyes used to dance with humour and affection as he and David played like otters in the swimming hole at home.

Silently, in his heart, he bid that boy farewell.

Will stepped forward. "Davy—"

But David was already turning away.

"Good-bye, Will," he said. And when he walked out the door, he left his old memories behind.

Euan insisted on going with them to Kinnell's townhouse, though he agreed to stay in the carriage.

"But if this plan of yours fails," he said as the carriage came to a halt at its destination, "and that bastard ends up putting a bullet in you out on Hampstead Heath, I won't rest until I've stuck a knife in his guts and ended his miserable existence."

"Not going to happen," Murdo replied without hesitation. "He'll jump at the chance to get out of this, and if he doesn't, he'll be the one to die on the heath, I can assure you of that."

His confidence seemed to ease Euan's tension, if only a little. The other man nodded his agreement and let them climb out of the carriage without any further protest.

The butler who answered the door was plainly expecting them. He showed them into a large, well-appointed study. It was big enough for both a huge desk and a round meeting table ringed with six chairs.

"Sir Alasdair will be with you directly," the butler said.

Once he had gone and closed the door behind himself, Murdo turned to David, elevating a brow. "Five guineas says he'll make us wait."

Despite everything—despite David's gut-deep worry about the prospect of Murdo facing Kinnell holding a loaded gun—Murdo himself seemed unconcerned. Amused even. His attitude infuriated and reassured David in equal measure.

Murdo was right about one thing. Kinnell did keep them waiting. It was almost twenty minutes before the man appeared. He was tidily turned out but did not look well. His face was grey with fatigue, drawn with worry. He couldn't have looked more different from Murdo if he'd tried.

During the wait, Murdo had sat himself down at the table with a book from one of the shelves that lined the room. He looked up at Kinnell's appearance in the doorway, but did not rise from his chair. In fact, he leaned back and propped his boots up on the table.

"Ah, Sir Alasdair! You grace us with your presence at last," he said. "But where is your second? Sir William, isn't it?"

David watched Kinnell's reaction to Murdo's comment, noting the minute signs of mingled irritation and fear—the tensing of his jaw, the warily watchful gaze.

"I prefer not to afford you an audience," he said.

"Very wise," Murdo agreed amiably. "You will not like some of what I have to say, and you certainly wouldn't want Sir William to hear it."

Kinnell walked round the table to select the chair farthest from Murdo before he sat down. "Sir William said you're prepared to apologise," he said, his tone clipped, businesslike. "Though only on certain conditions. What are the conditions?"

"Two things only," Murdo replied. "And both easily given. Firstly, I want Elizabeth. She will come away with me today when I leave this house. Secondly, I want you to divorce her."

Kinnell stared at him, plainly shocked. "You—you cannot ask that of me," he said at last.

Murdo leaned forward, his expression deadly serious. "I don't ask it. I demand it. If you want to get out of meeting me over pistols at dawn, you will agree." He gave an ugly smile. "After all, you know I'll win."

Kinnell flushed with anger. "That's an outrageous demand. I've every right to an apology. *You* insulted *me*! I am the innocent party here!"

Murdo reached across the table, seizing Kinnell's upper arm and yanking him forward till their faces were inches apart.

"You are not innocent!" he hissed. "You are a vicious bastard. You were vicious when you were a boy, and you're still vicious now. If you think I've forgotten the misery you heaped on me when I was smaller and weaker than you, you are very much mistaken." He pushed his face closer. "*Believe me*, nothing will give me greater pleasure than to put a bullet in you and remove you from the face of the earth. Whether or not you agree to my terms, your wife *will* be freed from this marriage. The only thing that's standing between you and your very imminent death is my wish to remove her from this house today. So I suggest you make the most of my very generous offer. I only have to wait another day or two to kill you, and I'm beginning to think it may be worth it."

When he released Kinnell, the other man fell back against his chair with a thud. His face was white with fear.

"How am I supposed to divorce her?" Kinnell mumbled at last.

"You can name me as her paramour. I won't protest. Given what happened at Culzeans last evening, you'll have ample evidence to support your case, not to mention the sympathy of your peers. Elizabeth will be maligned as an adulteress, of course"—he looked Kinnell directly in the eyes—"but I'm sure she'd rather live with disapproval than fear."

"It'll cost me a fortune."

Murdo shrugged. "You can afford it. Sell her jewellery. She doesn't need it anymore."

Kinnell's lips thinned, and his eyes glittered with malice. "You'll be maligned too. You'll be *ruined*. No one in polite society will acknowledge you again."

For an instant, Murdo paused. It wasn't long enough for Kinnell to notice, but David saw the brief hesitation, and he knew that in that instant Murdo counted the cost of all this to himself.

Then Murdo smiled.

"Touched as I am by your concern, I can assure you that you don't need to worry about me," he said coolly. "Now, if you are prepared to accept my offer, Mr. Lauriston here will draw up an agreement while we wait. If not, I'll be seeing you on Hampstead Heath at dawn. What's it to be?"

Chapter Nineteen

Whereas: the First Party acknowledges and admits that he has conducted adulterous relations with Lady Elizabeth Kinnell...

The ink was still wet on Murdo's and Kinnell's signatures when Kinnell turned on his heel and strode out of the study. When they followed him out a minute later, he was already gone. The butler, however, was hurrying towards them.

"Sir Alasdair has suggested that you wait for her ladyship in the hall," he said when he reached them. "If you would care to follow me, she will only be a few minutes."

And whereas: the Second Party acknowledges that he has subjected the said Lady Elizabeth Kinnell to cruel and inhumane treatment...

The butler wasn't wrong. Less than ten minutes later, Elizabeth appeared at the top of the stairs, walking behind a stiff-faced footman, her head bowed.

When she reached the bottom of the stairs and looked up, she gave a tremulous smile, only to flinch at David's indrawn breath and Murdo's hissed curse.

She was in a sorry state. One eye blackened, her mouth swollen and cut. God only knew what other injuries her clothing disguised. David could only hope that the child she carried was unharmed.

Now, therefore, the parties do hereby agree as follows...

It was just as well Kinnell had already removed himself, or David would have launched himself at the man, bad leg be damned. Suppressed rage had him clutching too tightly the agreement he'd just drawn up, and he had to force himself to loosen his grip. The agreement was for Elizabeth's protection, after all. He folded the papers and tucked them into the pocket of his coat before stepping forward.

"Elizabeth," he said. "I'm so sorry I led him to you."

"David." Her voice was little more than a breath. "Am I allowed to go with you?"

Her cautious hope was unbearable.

"Yes. Come on. Euan's waiting outside." He steered her across the hall towards the front door, Murdo following behind. A blank-faced footman swung the door open for them.

(First) The Second Party undertakes, entirely at his own cost, and within one month of execution hereof, to present a petition to the Court of Session in Edinburgh for dissolution of the marriage between the Second Party and the said Lady Elizabeth...

As they crossed the threshold of Kinnell's house, Elizabeth made an inarticulate noise somewhere between a sob and a sigh of relief, clutching at David's arm with gloveless fingers. It was only then that David realised that Kinnell was turning her out in the clothes she'd been wearing when she was snatched—no bonnet or gloves or cloak, just a plain muslin dress that was wholly inadequate for the biting March weather.

"Wait a moment," Murdo said behind them when Elizabeth shivered. He shrugged off his coat and tucked it about Elizabeth's shoulders. "That's better." He smiled. "Come on, the carriage is waiting a little way down the street."

As soon as Murdo's coachman saw them, he jumped down from his perch to open the carriage door, and Euan started forward from his seat in the corner.

"Thank God, Lizzie! Oh Christ, what has he done to you? Are you all right?"

She fell into his arms, half sobbing, half laughing, Murdo's coat listing off her narrow shoulders to land on the carriage floor as David and Murdo climbed in after her, slamming the door closed behind them.

"I'm fine," she said, taking Euan's face in her hands and pressing kisses all over it. "I'm fine. Don't look at the bruises, love, they don't matter. I'm here now."

"I'll kill him," Euan muttered, even as his arms came tightly about her.

"Don't think about him." She brushed his fair hair off his forehead in a tender gesture, as though he was the one that needed to be protected.

"How can I not?" Euan asked. "What if he does it again?"

The carriage lurched forward.

"That won't happen," Murdo assured him.

Euan sent him a bleak look. "How can you be so sure?"

David drew the agreement out of his coat pocket and held it out. "Read it."

(Second) The First Party will pay to the Second Party the sum of two hundred and fifty pounds Sterling within seven days of the date of execution hereof; the Second Party accepts that sum in full and final settlement of all claims he may have against the First Party howsoever arising.

Euan and Elizabeth bent their heads over the paper together. When they looked up, Elizabeth's eyes glistened with tears.

"I can't believe what you've done for me," she

whispered. She looked at Murdo. "Your reputation's ruined and over something you didn't even do."

Murdo smiled gently. "I am not entirely selfless. I gained something for myself from my actions."

"But two hundred and fifty pounds?" Euan said. "It'll take us forever to repay that."

Murdo looked at David, even as he answered Euan. "I don't want repaying. Two hundred and fifty pounds was nothing to what I've gained from this. Nothing at all."

Euan opened his mouth to argue, but before he could speak, David said, "Don't, Euan. Just accept it. For Elizabeth."

Euan fell silent.

"Will it work, David?" Elizabeth asked. "Is Kinnell bound by this?"

"It would be nigh on impossible to enforce," David replied. "But the point of it isn't to win a battle in court. It's a different sort of insurance."

"Because he admits to treating his wife cruelly?" Euan said. "Do you really think his reputation would be damaged by that?" He sounded sceptical.

"I think it would, a little," David said. "But that sort of dishonour pales in comparison to the damage that would be done to his reputation if it got out that he had failed to honour an agreement between gentlemen in order to avoid a duel."

Euan snorted his disgust, but the corners of his

mouth turned up as he did so.

Murdo turned to Elizabeth. "In short, you are free—as am I. Time to make the best of our lives, don't you think?"

Murdo prevailed upon Euan and Elizabeth to stay at the townhouse.

After he'd informed Liddle about their unexpected guests, the butler smoothly moved into action, dispatching a footman to have a bath readied for the lady and leading the tired, battered couple upstairs.

Within a few minutes of their return, David and Murdo were alone, hovering in the empty hallway, smiling at one another.

"You look exhausted," Murdo said.

"I feel like I could sleep for a week," David admitted. "I barely closed my eyes last night for worry."

"Let's go upstairs, then. I'm done in too."

Despite his eagerness to be fully alone with Murdo, David took the stairs slowly, not pushing himself too hard. Murdo noticed, of course.

"How's the leg?" he asked when they finally reached the top.

"All right," David said, leading the way to Murdo's bedchamber and pushing the door open. "It's better when I keep moving. Sitting around is the very worst thing for it, I think."

Murdo followed him inside, closing the door behind them. "Going back to legal practice doesn't sound like a good idea, then."

David was already halfway across the room, but at those words he turned. Murdo was leaning against the closed bedchamber door, watching him with an intent expression.

"I suppose—I suppose I'll have to make sure I take breaks. That sort of thing."

Murdo swallowed visibly. "Don't."

"What?"

Murdo gave a short laugh, letting his head knock back against the door. "I don't mean don't take breaks. I mean—don't go back."

"What?" David said again. God, he sounded stupid. *What? What?*

Murdo's expression grew determined, the look of a man undertaking a task he'd dreaded. "I don't want you to leave Laverock House," he said. "I want you to stay with me. Forever, if you'll have me."

David stared at him, too shocked to speak. The notion of having something he wanted so very badly—a lifetime beside the person he loved—was something he'd deemed impossible. And now Murdo was offering it to him. No, demanding it of him.

As he struggled to find words to reply, Murdo's determined expression faltered.

"You're always telling me that what we have can't last, that we have to be careful. Always reminding me that you'll be leaving me soon…"

David thought, suddenly, of Chalmers, and of the woman he had loved. The beloved he'd regretted leaving to die alone. And in that moment, David realised that he didn't want it to be like that for him and Murdo. He wanted to be at Murdo's side for the rest of their lives. He wanted to share it all, the good and the bad, the joy and the sorrow. He wanted to be able to lean on those broad, capable shoulders when he was weary, and to have Murdo lean on him.

"Love should not be denied."

They would have to be careful, of course they would, but they could surround themselves with the broad, green stretches of the Laverock estate. They could deal with any difficulties that came their way together, side by side. If they wanted it enough, it could be managed. And, oh, how David wanted it! He was done with self-sacrifice and guilt and martyred isolation. Murdo had saved him from that. Murdo had shown him he was no sinner, whatever the world might say.

"If you're worrying about me making plans to marry anyone behind your back, you needn't," Murdo added determinedly. "I'm done with that."

"You did rather burn your bridges on that one in Culzeans the other night."

"I knew exactly what I was doing." Murdo spoke intently, his dark gaze very direct, as though he needed David to understand this. "I saw Kinnell across the room, all pleased with himself, and right then I saw that I had this one chance. Not just to save Elizabeth but to save *myself*. To rid myself of all the things that had been chaining me down—my engagement, my father, the expectations that attach to a man like me." He gave an uncertain smile. "I burned all those bridges, David, and in that moment, I think I felt free for the first time in my life." He stepped forward, closing the distance between them, touching David's face with gentle fingers. "Come home with me."

"I want to," David said, returning Murdo's earnest gaze. "But I have to be sure—have you really thought about what you're giving up? You once told me you wanted everything the world had to offer, not just male lovers, but a wife and family of your own—"

"And I was wrong," Murdo interrupted. "I was lost back then. Oh, I didn't *think* I was lost. I thought I was going to have it all. Two lives, one that would be respectable and safe, and a secret one of pleasure and vice." He gave a rueful laugh. "I thought you were naïve, till you made me see that the life I'd always wanted—the two lives I'd wanted—didn't amount to anything at all. I wasn't going to have it all. I was going to have nothing." He paused. "You saved me from that."

David opened his mouth to say, *And you saved me.* To tell Murdo all the ways in which he'd saved David. But the words died in his throat. For now, anyway, because Murdo was looking at him in a way that made speech impossible. Murdo Balfour, who'd spent his life hiding his true feelings behind an amused little smile and a single crooked brow, was looking at David with desperate, undisguised hope.

"So you'll come back with me, then?" he whispered. "To Laverock?"

For a moment, his question hung in the air between them. Till David somehow managed to unlock his throat and make his mouth work again and gave Murdo his answer.

"I will."

Epilogue

One year later

David had the coachman stop the carriage and let him out at the top of the hill. It was too beautiful a day to sit in the carriage for this last and best part of the journey. By getting out here, he could walk a couple of miles over the ridge before dropping down to the glen through a path in the woods that backed onto Laverock House.

David watched the carriage rumble on without him. It would arrive with no passenger, only an economically packed trunk of clothes, three boxes of books and papers he'd picked up from Murdo's Edinburgh townhouse during his brief visit, and a clootie dumpling wrapped up in muslin cloth. This last, his favourite boyhood treat, came from his mother's kitchen in Midlauder. She'd spent the last three days fussing over him and sent him home not only with the pudding but—despite his protests that his leg was quite better—with a pot of her homemade liniment which, she told him, he was to make sure to keep using every day.

It was a bit of a climb to the top of the next hill, but after that it would be level walking for a good while, and, anyway, it felt good to David to stretch his legs after all the hours he'd spent in the carriage. These days he relished the small discomforts that came with such exertions, the faint burn in his calves and the rasp of his breath as his lungs worked harder.

By the end of the climb up, David's knee ached a bit, but only a bit. He sat down on a large, flat boulder to rest, giving his knee a brisk rub while he looked out at the place he'd come to call home—at the tumbling river with its black, rocky teeth, and at the hills, dominated by brownish bracken now, but soon to brighten with the advent of spring. Above his head, a skylark—a laverock—wheeled and plummeted, and David tracked its bold, sweeping dance for several minutes till it finally disappeared into a copse of trees.

Rising from his perch, he began to walk along the ridge, his eyes drinking in the familiar views as he walked. It was good to be back here, in the country. He loved the almost-lonely beauty of his new home. Edinburgh was elegant, but it teemed with people. Returning to the city for the first time in almost a year, he'd been struck by how busy it felt, how noisy and dirty and muddled it was. He'd finished up the business matters he'd needed to deal with as soon as he possibly could, eager to come home.

It would be another half year before he needed to leave Laverock again, though the occasional trip was unavoidable. He was, after all, Lord Murdo Balfour's man of business now—and, increasingly, an investor in his own right. And it wasn't as though Murdo could attend to these matters by himself anymore. The people round here didn't know the details of the scandal that had driven their aristocratic neighbour back to Perthshire, banishing him from the polite drawing rooms of London forever, but they whispered about it. Most particularly about the married woman who had broken his heart. The woman he'd fought a duel over, no less. It was why Lord Murdo had engaged Mr. Lauriston as his permanent man of business, they said, since he could no longer show his face in London.

It was why, they whispered, he would never marry.

The story was scandalous, romantic, and most importantly, verifiable. And Murdo played his part of new gentleman farmer beautifully. Not that it required any effort—it was, after all, what he'd always wanted to do. He would happily spend the rest of his life exiled in Perthshire, managing his new estate.

He had agreed, though, to accompany David on his next trip, a visit to Lancashire in the autumn to inspect a new factory Murdo was financing. While they were there, they'd be looking in on the MacLennans. Euan and Elizabeth were married now and fond parents to a fine, strong boy: Patrick David MacLennan. Murdo wanted to stop at the Lake District on the way back to Scotland. There was good hill walking there, he said, and scenery to rival Laverock Glen, though David found that difficult to believe.

David stopped when he reached the end of the ridge. The edge of the woods that led to the house was just a few feet away, but David wanted one last look at the glen below before he took the path down the hill.

He was standing there in the weak spring sunshine, his open coat flapping in the wind and his hat in his hand, when a shout roused him from his reverie.

"There you are!"

It was Murdo, emerging from the woods. David felt his smile grow, felt the face-aching broadness of it. It was a mirror of that rare and wonderful smile that Murdo reserved for him alone and that Murdo wore now.

"You bastard!" the other man exclaimed as he drew closer. He was laughing, though, white teeth flashing. "I came out to meet the carriage for our grand reunion to find nothing but a *pudding* to greet me!"

The laughter that bubbled out of David came from deep inside him, like water from an underground spring. It burbled up and fell from his lips as he walked into Murdo's arms, stopped only by the firm press of the other man's mouth as they came together in a fiercely joyful kiss.

"That's better," Murdo murmured when they finally pulled apart, and the soft words tingled against David's lips.

"I'm a day early," David said. "I didn't think you'd be at the house, or I'd've stayed with the carriage."

"What can I say?" Murdo grinned. "I must've had a premonition that my beloved would get home today."

My beloved.

"I missed you," David said.

"And I you."

They smiled at one another for a long, perfect moment, right there, at the edge of the woods. At the edge of the broad, green stretch that surrounded their home.

"Come on," Murdo said. "Let's go back to the house."

He took David's hand and tugged him towards the start of the woodland path.

Murdo clambered over the stile first, and when David stepped up after him, he said, "How's the leg?"

David glared at him. Murdo still asked that question every day. Force of habit, Murdo claimed. "It's good," David replied firmly. "I got out of the carriage at the top of Bank's Hill and did the climb up here with no bother."

"None at all?" Murdo sounded sceptical.

David sent him a defiant look. "Just the barest ache at the very end. Nothing a five-minute rest didn't cure." He jumped from the stile step to the ground to make his point.

Murdo raised one brow in a perfect arch—cool and amused—the eternal aristocrat. "Did your mother give you any more liniment? I think I'd better give you a rubdown if your leg's been aching."

David couldn't suppress a grin at that. "As it happens, she did."

"She's an excellent woman, your mother," Murdo observed.

"She is," David agreed. "She's the one who sent that clootie dumpling you saw in the carriage earlier. It's her prized recipe and her dearest wish is that you'll give it a try."

"That monstrous pudding?" Murdo looked appalled. "That's your mother's clootie dumpling? Good lord, David, it weighs a *ton*! What's in it? Rocks?" He shook his head, wrinkling his nose. "I'll leave the clootie dumpling to you to dispose of, if you don't mind. You're the one with the sweet tooth."

"Oh come on, you have to at least *try* it," David wheedled. "If I write and tell her that no less a personage than Lord Murdo Balfour ate her dumpling, she'll be able to crow to all the neighbours for weeks."

Murdo reached for David's hand, entwining their fingers together. His eyes danced with humour. "All right, I'll try it," he said, tugging David towards the path. "I promise."

"I'll hold you to that," David replied, enjoying the warmth of Murdo's hand in his and the companionable bump of their shoulders as they made their way down the path.

"Honestly," Murdo sighed. "The things I do for love."

The End

Read the previous two instalments of David and Murdo's story in Books One and Two of the Enlightenment series, *Provoked* and *Beguiled*

PROVOKED

Tormented by his forbidden desires for other men and the painful memories of the childhood friend he once loved, lawyer David Lauriston tries to maintain a celibate existence while he forges his reputation in Edinburgh's privileged legal world.

But then, into his repressed and orderly life, bursts Lord Murdo Balfour.

Cynical, hedonistic and utterly unapologetic, Murdo could not be less like David. And as appalled as David is by Murdo's unrepentant self-interest, he cannot resist the man's sway. Murdo tempts and provokes David in equal measure, forcing him to acknowledge his physical desires.

But Murdo is not the only man distracting David from his work. Euan MacLennan, the brother of a convicted radical David once represented, approaches David to beg him for help. Euan is searching for the government agent who sent his brother to Australia on a convict ship, and other radicals to the gallows. Despite knowing it may damage his career, David cannot turn Euan away.

As their search progresses, it begins to look as though

the trail may lead to none other than Lord Murdo Balfour, and David has to wonder whether it's possible Murdo could be more than he seems. Is he really just a bored aristocrat, amusing himself at David's expense, or could he be the agent provocateur responsible for the fate of Peter MacLennan and the other radicals?

Beguiled

Two years after his last encounter with cynical nobleman Lord Murdo Balfour, David Lauriston accidentally meets him again in the heart of Edinburgh.

King George IV is about to make his first visit to Edinburgh and Murdo has been sent North by his politician father to represent his aristocratic family at the celebrations.

David and Murdo's last parting was painful—and on Murdo's part, bitter—but Murdo's feelings seem to have mellowed in the intervening years. So much so, that he suggests to David that they enjoy each other's company during Murdo's stay in the capital.

Despite his initial reservations, David cannot put Murdo's proposal from his mind, and soon find himself at Murdo's door—and in his arms.

But other figures from David's past are converging on the city, and as the pomp and ceremony of the King's visit unfolds around them, David is drawn into a chain of events that will threaten everything: his career, his wellbeing, and the fragile bond that, despite David's best intentions, is growing between him and Murdo.

Thank you for taking the time to read this story—I do hope you enjoyed it. I'm very appreciative of any reviews—good or bad—that readers are kind enough to take the time to post, whether at retailer sites, on social media or on blogs or reviews.

If you want to sign up for my newsletter, you can do that on my website, where you can also find out more about my books. If you want to connect with me, you can do that on Twitter, Facebook and Goodreads.

Website: www.joannachambers.com
Twitter: @ChambersJoanna
Facebook: facebook.com/joanna.chambers.58

Titles by Joanna Chambers

The Enlightenment Series
Provoked
Beguiled
Enlightened
Seasons Pass
Unnatural

Porthkennack Series (Riptide)
A Gathering Storm

Other novel length titles
The Dream Alchemist
Unforgivable
The Lady's Secret

Novellas and Short Stories
Humbug (a Christmas tale)
Rest and Be Thankful
(appeared in the *Comfort and Joy* anthology)
Introducing Mr. Winterbourne
(appeared in the *Another Place in Time* anthology)
Mr. Perfect's Christmas
(appeared in the *Wish Come True* anthology)

Made in the USA
Middletown, DE
17 June 2020